A Good Man

Bardy Thomas

ISBN:978-1-9998181-3-5

Published by Write Side Left Ltd

DT6 3AG

www.WriteSideLeft.com

PART ONE

Chapter 1. Max

'I've got to go at the end of the week.'

'That's fine.'

'The girls will be on half-term and I can't leave it all to Howard.'

'No problem.'

Derek was relieved. His sister was well-meaning but he felt obliged to perform, to show just enough grief, and a great deal of backbone. He knew she was afraid he'd slump in a chair with the whisky bottle, as their father had done; not such a bad plan, Derek thought.

'When are you going back to school?'

'I'm not sure.'

'Why don't you start after half-term? It will give you something to do,' she said, as though work was a pleasant diversion, an absorbing hobby.

'Yes, I probably will.'

'Good.'

Derek sat at his desk. There were untidy piles of papers —invoices, funeral costs, insurance claims. He flicked through a few, but couldn't settle. He'd see to it another time. The photograph on his desk was of Chris and him standing, skis in hand. They were at Big White in British Columbia; her dad had taken the picture. Their first visit, a picture book landscape — Chris had turned out to be a genius skier. He'd had a job to keep up…

'Did you hear me?'

'What?'

'I'm going shopping, Derek. I'll get you stocked up before I go.'

Christ, she treats me like an invalid or an imbecile, he thought.

'Why don't you make that phone call while I'm out? I'll blow the horn when I'm back so you can help me up.'

'What?'

'Call school.'

'Oh, yes.'

It was a relief to be alone in the flat. It was the first time since the funeral. He was grateful to his sister but she could go as soon as she liked. He was calmer alone. He wandered round the small flat, and looked at things as though he had never seen them before: his desk in the corner; the bookshelves with the photographs; the faded sofa. He made himself a coffee, turned on the radio, and turned it off again. The uncompromising confidence of the presenters undermined him. It was like being in a dream where everyone knew the script and he was in the wrong costume. He was exposed by them, and preferred silence.

Standing with his coffee, he stared at the bookshelves. The novels were in alphabetical order. They'd always read the same ones so they could talk about them. Oversized books on Art and Dance were at the bottom and there was a special shelf for Shakespeare. As he gazed unseeingly at the shelves, his thoughts went back to school. This was the term he would have to introduce the Form Six play. They always read and studied it first, and then rehearsed in the summer, in preparation for parents' evening.

He pulled out *The Merchant of Venice*. Hudson had expressed a preference for *Twelfth Night*. That would have been a safe choice, but he'd done it before, in two different London schools; he wanted a change. He became absorbed — 'In sooth I know not why I am so sad…/Thou knowest that all my fortunes are at sea'— when a car horn interrupted him.

The following morning, whilst Debbie was packing, he phoned the headmaster and arranged to go in and see him in the afternoon.

Hudson's office was on the first floor of the main house, in what had been the library when it had been a private dwelling. Derek knocked, and responded to the booming response.

'Come in, sit down. How very good to see you, how are you feeling? A very moving service, a good chap, he spoke well.'

Derek had only been in this room once before, at his interview. There would only be one more visit. Books covered two walls from floor to ceiling. Derek suspected that most of them were facsimiles; he was equally convinced that any that contained real pages had never been opened by the present incumbent.

'Sister still looking after you? Having to behave yourself?'

What did Hudson mean? What spurious opinion had he formed about Derek over the last three years?

'Yes, yes, she's still at the flat.'

'Now, what can I do for you?'

'Well, I was thinking I could resume my duties after half-term.'

'Splendid, that's splendid. I was worried you were going to tell me you were moving on — pastures new and all that.'

Is that what he wanted him to do, Derek wondered?'Now, I can set that in motion right away, I had a "supply" lined up but that's not a problem.'

'If you're sure.'

'Of course I'm sure. Now, there's a new boy joining your Form Six … bit of an oddball; father an international lawyer, based in New York; mother in Argentina with a polo player; boy gets bandied about. There was an incident at his last school, so time for a fresh start and all that. Trouble is we've got him here now, just arrived, and they want us to look after him during the break. All the house masters are away — winter sports, you know how it is — so wondered if you could take him on. Take your mind off things a bit. Anyway, have a think, discuss it with your sister and let me know. Tomorrow will be OK.'

Debbie was ready to leave by the time Derek got back.

'How did that go?'

'Fine, yes I'll start back after half-term.'

'Why don't you come back with me for the week? Howard can take a few days off, it would set you up.' He declined, said he'd got to get used to it sometime, and didn't mention that a boy might stay.

It was only a short walk from his flat to the main house, but Derek collected Max in the car on Saturday morning. Hudson was standing with the boy on the front steps.

Derek explained the car. 'Going into town to get pizzas for lunch.'

'Splendid.'

The boy was silent.

'Have you got everything?'

Max was carrying a small canvas bag. He was dressed in a crumpled grey suit, school uniform, and — despite the aura of wealth about him, which showed in his haircut, his lightly tanned skin and expensive shoes — he had a hopeless look; the pedigree puppy that no one chooses because they prefer its lively mongrel kennel mate. He was a slender boy of thirteen, a cross-country runner, or a fly half in the rugby team; boys had to be sporty in this school. Derek had his hand on the passenger seat door when the boy got in the back. Derek shrugged — used to chauffeurs, he presumed. He acknowledged Hudson, who was already on his way back inside.

The pizza place was a fifteen-minute silent drive into town. When he pulled up outside, he asked Max what he would like on his pizza. There was no answer from the back. Derek looked round. It wasn't that the boy looked nervous; rather, his blankness or absence made Derek nervous.

'Come in and have a look at the menu.' Max leaned over to get his bag,

'It's all right, you can leave that.' He brought it, just the same. Derek explained that there was thin crust, or thick crust, or filled crust, and about a dozen different toppings, and Max now looked in such a panic that Derek thought he might bolt.

'Shall I choose for both of us then?' Max nodded furiously.

Back at the flat, Derek served up the pizzas, asked if he'd like ketchup or pickle, and began to get annoyed by the boy's lack of communication. Eventually Derek stopped trying and they ate in silence. Afterwards Max asked if he could go to his room and read. Derek thought about asking him to do the clearing up, but was actually quite relieved that the boy would disappear for a while.

'I'm glad you are a reader. Have a look on the shelves — you might find something you like.' Max stood in front of the shelves, Derek washed up, and when he returned to the living room ten minutes later, Max was still in the same position.

'Help yourself if there's anything you fancy.'

Max turned to Derek. 'I've got a book.'

'OK, off you go then.'

Max went into the small spare bedroom and closed the door. Four and a half hours later, Derek knocked and asked if he would like some supper and would he like to watch a film? There was no answer, but in five minutes he appeared in the kitchen.

'What have you been reading?'

'I fell asleep.'

'Good lad — do you want to choose a film while I cook these sausages? Do you like sausages?'

'Yes, thank you.' After a silent supper Derek found *Pan's Labyrinth* on the coffee table.

'That one's in Spanish. you know.'

'Yes.'

'I mean it is the original — no subtitles.'

'That's OK.'

The film Derek knew was about a thirteen-year old girl, who has a pregnant mother and a sadistic father, a Falangist in post-civil-war Spain. The girl escapes into the mythical world of an old Labyrinth. Derek wondered what it was about the film that resonated with Max, who had clearly seen it before.

In the days that followed, Max kept to his room, appearing only for meals. Whether the boy read, or watched films on his tablet, Derek knew not. His own sorrow, and Max's deep gloom, somehow struck an odd chord. Debbie called him every day. He lied and said Max had come a couple of days after she had left. She thought it strange that Hudson had suggested he looked after the boy on his own, but believed it typical of the man's selfishness. She suggested that they got out into the fresh air, away from books and films. So, after lunch towards the end of the week, Derek asked Max if he would like to go on a hike, see a bit of the countryside. Perhaps they could go down to the sea; he presumed Max was a stranger to this part of the world.

The school lay in its own estate, about two miles from the coast — as the seagull flies), with no roads in between. They set off silently, along a muddy track between two tall hedges. The sky was grey. Glutinous mud attached itself to Max's trainers and made each step heavier than the last. When the path widened out and the surface was stony, he tried to scrape off the mud with clumps of grass and leaves. Derek said he could put them in the washing machine when they got back, but Max did not reply, only continued his efforts. The road wound downhill. At one point, they came across a hollow in the rock — a natural amphitheatre.

'Perhaps we could put on an outdoor performance of a play here?' They paused and Max ventured in.

The rocks were moss covered and water ran down to spongy ground. On ledges, there were ferns and some early flowers.

'It smells of fox,' Max said. Derek couldn't pick up the scent.

'It's a bit wet, we'd have to do the play in summer.'

'*A Midsummer Night's Dream* then?' suggested Max.

'Who would you like to play?'

'Nobody.'

He replied as though "nobody" were a character. They left the grotto and silently continued their hike. As the sea came into view, the track descended steeply to the stony beach. The school had put up a rope rail to help walkers down the slope; it was wet and mini-landslides had to be negotiated. The final thirty feet was an abseil on a knotted rope that would have deterred all but the most athletic. Once down, Max set off towards where rocks spread out into the sea at one end of the long shoreline. The beach was shingle, into which each step sank, making walking arduous.

'How far do you want to go?' shouted Derek from behind.

'I don't mind.'

He called back without turning or altering his pace. Once he reached the reef, he began staring and poking and testing with fingers the soft and hard inhabitants, and Derek saw himself at twelve years old peering into worlds on Westward Ho beach, near where he stayed with his grandparents each summer; where the sun always shone, puddings were served with Bird's custard, and his grandfather played jazz on vinyl. This boy, as far as he knew, had grown up in capital cities in Australia, Malaysia, America North and South, the Caymans and other tax havens; the fascination of rock pools must dwell deep in human psychology.

Derek found a flat rock at the top of the shingle and sat and watched the boy, who was totally immersed in his task. Max would carefully lift stones or shells or small creatures, from the pool he was working on, examine them for a few minutes and — following private criteria — either put them back in the pool or place them on a rock, before moving on to the next.

The solid grey sky was breaking up; there was no blue; yet clouds were discernible — clouds on clouds. He should have had a child with Chris, a boy like this, looking like his mother. The time had never seemed right. He would have been a solace now.

Derek approached and asked what he'd found. Max visibly jumped.

'Just stuff.'

'Can I see?'

'If you like.'

'Do you like?'

Max didn't answer. The rock had about a dozen separate items — shells, stones, seaweed, dead crabs, the usual stuff.

'It's getting on a bit. We should probably set off, to be back before dark. Do you want to take these with you?'

Max just stared. He couldn't read this boy. Terms were bandied about in the staff room such as 'damaged' or 'autistic' or 'on the spectrum'. Derek found them meaningless. Who wasn't damaged, to a greater or lesser extent? He pulled a plastic bag from his pocket and handed it to Max. They stood looking at each other, Max clutching the bright orange Sainsbury's bag.

'If you want to go on, I'll catch you up,' Max said.

Derek turned and set off, wondering what was so private about putting a collection of seashells into a plastic bag.

He caught up and they trudged back, mostly in silence. The sky had corrugated over and it was darker than was to be expected for the time of day. Max was ahead and started up the rope. It was an awkward climb. He was nearing the top when he slipped several feet, one hand arrested by a knot, the other clutching his bag like an orange balloon. Left to right the balloon took him, in a swing away from the rock and back again. A more athletic boy might have been showing off but Max was panicking. Derek ploughed forward through the shingle to steady the end of the rope.

'Drop the bag and grab the rope.'

He continued to dangle.

'You must climb, Max.'

Still clutching the rope knot with his left hand and dangling twelve feet up, he began to circle the wrist of his right hand in the air. He was trying to slip the bag up his arm, in order to free his hand to climb.

'Drop the bag!' Derek shouted again. Still ignoring him, the boy succeeded in getting the bag suspended from his elbow and cautiously began to climb the last few feet to the path. Once there, he set off, without waiting for Derek to join him.

When Derek eventually caught up, muddy and irritated, he too did not even bother to attempt conversation. Back at the flat, after a shower and a surreptitious whisky, he asked Max if he would like bacon and beans for supper or would he prefer to go into town for fish and chips?

'I don't mind.'

'You choose,' Derek said, surprisingly fiercely.

'Fish and chips.'

'Great, that's what I fancy too.'

Progress.

He sat at his desk in his suit; a scruffy blackbird sat on the wall outside; he checked his watch. It was two minutes since he had last checked.

He had been five years old when his mother died, and he had been deemed too young for sad events. His nine-year-old sister took him to a neighbour's, where he was to 'play' whilst she went with their father, and uncles and aunts, to the church. He remembered sitting at a kitchen table and being given a jigsaw puzzle. The picture was of a huge white cat. He'd never seen a jigsaw before and the old lady who was looking after him showed him how to look for the edging pieces. She had warts on her hands.

When his father died, Derek was travelling in Argentina. He didn't have the money for a special flight back and his sister said it was best for him to continue his travels; so he did.

His sister was in the kitchen now, drinking coffee, tidying up. His 'in-laws' would arrive soon. He checked his watch again. When the doorbell rang, Debbie buzzed them in from the kitchen. The blackbird, a female this time, equally scruffy, poked about in the flowerbed.

Paul and Susan looked too big for his flat. Susan was breathing heavily.

'Don't you have elevators in this country?'

'Sorry. Sit down, please.' Susan looked around. It was hard to believe this was Chris's mother.

'Good morning, Derek. How are you feeling?' Paul was wiry, tough, twenty years a steeplejack. Chris took after him physically. Debbie came through and offered coffee, Derek suggested something stronger, both declined. Derek blushed; he had forgotten they were Methodist and didn't touch alcohol.

There was another ring on the doorbell. 'That will be the funeral cars.' Susan, who mumbled that it was hardly worth coming up, led the way down the narrow staircase. The funeral directors had arranged everything.

The man taking the service had called on Derek. He described himself as a Celebrant, and asked him questions about Chris. He gave him the facts. She was brought up in Canada, she came to London to train as a dancer, she went to the Laban Centre in Deptford; he was at Goldsmiths.

He couldn't remember the name of his original date; they were meeting in The Dog and Bell. It was crowded. Whoever she was wasn't there anyway. He fought his way to the bar.

'Excuse me, I was next.'

The barman was nonplussed. Derek indicated that he should go ahead and serve the young woman. She gave her order for four pints, and turned and thanked Derek.

'Do you need some help with those?'

'You'll lose your place.'

'I'm not in a hurry.' She took two glasses and led the way to a table; he followed with the other two.

'Thanks. I'm Chris by the way.'

He put the pints down; there were two guys and another woman at the table.

'Why don't you join us?'

'Thanks, I'll do that. I'll just get a pint.' That was it, simple. They talked all evening, shouting over the noise of the pub. She was lively, intelligent, humorous, challenging and very attractive, hair blondish, scraped back, blue eyes with an appealing cast. They were a group of friends from the dance school, he wasn't interrupting anything, and his forgotten date hadn't turned up.

They married when she was twenty-six. She was dancing, mostly abroad, usually Germany. He went too, and taught English as a foreign language. Her roles got smaller; at thirty-two she retired. They came back to England. Six years in London, various teaching jobs, a move to this seaside town to get away, and then the leukaemia.

Was that the sort of thing he wanted? No, Derek didn't want to speak at the service. He was frightened of speaking, frightened of crying. But now he heard it coming back at him from this tall stranger, he wished he had been braver.

Her coffin was on the bier, a few feet in front of him. He had chosen it from a catalogue; it was so random, and he had needed her to agree. The chapel was full of mourners. She had been involved with a gym and sports group, people he hardly knew.

'Christabel was much loved in the community, a keen gardener, stalwart of the tennis club...' He hadn't told him that; he never called her Christabel. He hated the word 'stalwart'. A 'verruca of the tennis club' popped into his mind. He stopped listening.

The polished wood on her coffin was like a pre-war sideboard in front of guesthouse-beige curtains. She was in that box, his wife. Soon she would go through the curtains. Ella Fitzgerald was singing the Cole Porter song; 'I love Paris'. They had been there, in Paris, only four weeks ago. The curtains opened, the coffin moved slowly — and she was gone. He needed to swallow but something stuck, a cricket ball in his throat. No one could move until he did, people stood and shuffled. Someone, a woman, Monica (a woman from the school), took his arm and walked him out of the chapel. Then he was with Chris's parents in the taxi. Paul's hand was on his shoulder.

'It was a good service Derek, you did well.'

The room at the local hotel was full of people in black. Wine was laid out, and tea, and plates of ham and egg sandwiches. A colleague brought him a whisky from the bar.

'You all right, old man? This'll help.'

'Thank you.'

The headmaster assailed him. 'Take your time Derek, after half-term eh? Or take the whole term.' And there was an onslaught of helpfulness from colleagues' wives.

'You must come round.'

'Dinner next week?'

'I'll bring you supper.'

'John's just started playing golf, why don't you join him?'

'Do you play bridge?'

The sandwiches were finished. There were fewer people in black. Derek sought his parents-in-law, who were staying at the hotel for a few days, and arranged to meet them the following day. On his way to the lavatory he passed a side door — a delivery entrance — and slipped out.

The town had been built two miles from the coast, a mix of superior eighteenth-century houses and more ordinary Victorian dwellings and shopfronts. He turned off the high street and walked through narrow lanes of former workers' houses, vaguely in the direction of the sea. It was the first week of February. A quote slipped into his mind: 'the very worst of nature's might'. But it wasn't the very worst really, it was only cold-ish and damp-ish. Derek had left his overcoat at the hotel, but he didn't notice. He wanted to move, to feel the air (fresh or not), to hear the gulls shriek. He left the streets and set off on a dog walker's path towards the ocean.

A sudden call, aggressive, made him jump. He looked in the direction it came from, and could only see a few sheep huddled against a fence. Not for the first time he'd mistaken a sheep's baa for a human call. He'd heard that certain dialects contained sounds of their districts. Here the local dialect was soft; in London they would have mocked it for slowness of mind. He liked it here. Chris was the one with itchy feet. Having broken with the city, she was hankering after something even more remote. He could hear rubber on tarmac above him. The path ran beneath a dual carriageway. The supports of the overpass were covered in graffiti — big blocks of paint swirling in indecipherable language, skilfully executed.

A stage set for a modern dance, *Stadtansitch*: Chris the female principal, a big chance for her. The Stuttgart Ballet, a magnificent opening night, a standing ovation. The accident was during the third performance. Chris executed a particularly athletic leap and her leading man tripped and failed to catch her as the audience gasped. The pair bravely got to their feet and finished as though they had no pain. Derek was backstage when she hobbled off. A break in her Achilles tendon, it signalled the end. There was a repair and some small roles, but it was the end.

The path stopped in a caravan park: rows of mobile homes, each with a calling card patio with picket fence surround, pastel shades, individualised but only to a limited extent. The place was deserted, as though the inhabitants had been given time to put their homes in order before fleeing — what? Only winter.

Perhaps returning home had been a mistake. Life on one salary in London was difficult, but their changed circumstances affected Derek the most. He resented their dingy rented flat; the budget checking; the dependence of 'offers'. Chris grieved for her lost career. She tried teaching (Saturday mornings in a community hall in Clapham) but she hated it. She put on weight, guzzled anti-depressants, and lay on the sofa all day in their miserable flat until Derek returned from work. Then he came up with the idea of a move.

He reached the shore. A mist of fine rain began to soak through his jacket without him noticing. The waves met the shingle with a whisper. Further up the beach there was a figure with two dogs. His phone bleeped. 'Where are you? Are you OK?' He replied apologetically. He was OK, gone for a walk, would be home later. It wasn't easy walking in his leather shoes; they sank in the shingle. It took him half an hour to reach the rocks at the end of the beach. He'd passed the woman with her dogs, who'd nodded to him. He thought he knew her face. Small communities were like that. Certain people were very visible; others could live a lifetime without ever being noticed.

The rain was heavier now, and with it came sudden gusts; as he turned back, he was walking into the wind. 'Give not a windy night a rainy morrow'. Most people's earworms were tunes; his were words. He tried, but failed, to avoid the grey clay slime that crept from the cliffs, as though trying to colonise the shore, and spoil the games played there. His shoes clotted, and were probably ruined by the time he reached the concrete pavement that served as the promenade. He passed wooden huts that in the summer sold beach paraphernalia. They were now shut, with peeling paint and redundant signs advertising '99s' and 'hot dogs'. He got a whiff of fish and chips and realised he was hungry, immensely hungry. He'd had no breakfast, nothing at the hotel, and now — he looked at his watch — it was four-thirty and more or less dark. The shop was just closing but served Derek what they had left in the fryer: two small cod and a mountain of chips. He sat on a tall stool at a shelf and was brought an unordered cup of tea.

They'd had a good year, before the diagnosis. Chris had reduced her medication, taken up yoga, perhaps a little too neurotically, but she was happier and Derek therefore felt they might make a go of it. She joined a tennis club and played while he was at school.

Derek took the call. 'Could you and Mrs Baker call in at the surgery this evening?' He didn't even know she'd been to the doctor's. It crossed his mind that she might be pregnant, though they'd not planned a baby. Chris assured him she was not. She said they'd taken some blood when she called for her medication. Something must have shown up. She'd go alone, she said, but she didn't.

After that there was eighteen months, some of their best times, and all of their worst. They'd travelled again, loved again, found pleasure in small things, hoped and believed in the possibility of a cure. One day near the end, they were in Paris, and she said she knew, and it was OK; she just had to get used to dying.

Sitting over his fish and chips, he couldn't hold on. His clothes strained their drink to the floor, where it joined with the clay from the beach; a dirty stream ran across the white tiled floor. His chips grew cold with tears.

'I'm closing up now.' Derek started, turned on his stool to the counter and caught his plate in his sleeve, the remains of his meal combined with the muddy stream.

'You're in a bit of a state, mate.'

'I'm sorry.'

'Here. For your face.' The proprietor came round and handed Derek a wad of napkins.

'Oh yes.'

'I'll hold your glasses.'

'Thank you.' Derek wiped his face and blew his nose and said he was sorry again and could he help clear up?

'Where do you live?'

'At the school, St Edmund's … I'm so sorry … I've just been to my wife's funeral.' The tears began again.

The proprietor stepped over the debris, locked the door and pulled the blind down. 'I'll deal with this later. Mind where you tread.' He led him out through a back door to where his van was parked.

'I'll take you home.'

'We were thinking, we'd do a painted cloth of the Rialto?'

'How stupid.'

'I beg your pardon?'

'Sorry, sorry, Paul. I was thinking of something else.'

'Well what? I'm sure the art department will do its best to oblige,' Paul said.

'No, no, not about the set, about something else entirely.'

Paul pursed his lips. 'Right, well, we'll get back to you with some sketches.' He sashayed, muttering, from the ballroom — re-designated as the school theatre — followed by his small group of protégés.

How stupid, he'd been thinking, to choose *The Merchant of Venice*. He'd been careful to select a play with no great romantic tragedy, but had not thought about other difficulties. Racism? Homosexuality? Gender issues? He hadn't passed it by Hudson, who'd be bound to object. He began to wonder if he really was ready for school life again. He'd liked teaching in London, persuading himself he was making a difference. This was not his sort of school. It had been a mistake; he didn't fit. Now he was alone again, perhaps it was time to move on.

'Books out. You'll see your name against the character you are to read on this sheet.' Derek handed the pile of paper to the first boy. 'Take one and pass on.'

'Sir, I don't want to read Portia.'

'Why not, Daniel?' Dr Hudson was a progressive headmaster and surnames were no longer the norm.

'Because she's wet, Sir, and I want to play Antonio.'

Portia is one of Shakespeare's most intelligent women, she is the centre of the whole plot. Without her, there would be no play.'

'My voice is breaking, Sir.'

'May I have another volunteer then?'

Silence. Scorn from Daniel being far worse than disappointing Mr Baker. A hand went up; it was Max.

'Yes, Max?'

'I'll play her, Sir.'

There were suppressed giggles and Derek foresaw a disastrous production if he allowed this strange, silent boy to play the heroine.

'Thank you, Max. I don't know about your acting ability but please read the part in this lesson.'

The first boys began reading their characters; the interpretation was flat and lifeless.

'Agoo…'

'Ague.'

'What's that mean, Sir?'

'Illness, a fever.' The boy continued, but there was a sudden outburst of laughter and a boy at the back went bright red and threw a ruler at the reader. Derek raised his voice to regain control.

'What was all that about?' There was no response. 'I want to know.'

'Andrew, Sir.' He was the one who had thrown the ruler. They had just come to 'my wealthy *Andrew* docked in sand'. Andrew was a pupil whose parents were known in the boys' parlance to be 'mega-rich'. Derek, warming to the wit and warmth of classroom banter, calmed them down and began a discussion about ships and trade, modern and ancient, and the class passed pleasantly without getting to the 'lady richly left' and the love interest. He could prepare himself for that at their next meeting. 'Homework is to read Act One, Scenes One to Three, twice.'

'Sir?'

'Yes, Daniel.'

'I will play Portia if you really want me to.'

Derek paused. Daniel was a good actor, physically suitable to play the young woman, and he'd had him in mind from the start. Having Daniel on board would oil the wheels; he was popular and dominant. Max was looking out of the window.

'I'm sorry Daniel, I'll have to audition you both.'

Daniel laughed and he and his gang pushed to be first out of the door.

How stupid, he thought, to choose *The Merchant of Venice*.

Later, he defrosted one of the many ready meals left for him by his sister, and without much enthusiasm opened his computer to watch a film of *The Merchant*, with Al Pacino playing Shylock. He had no doubt that this production would be being played on the laptops of Form Six in place of the reading prep he had set. One of the first shots was of a crowd on the Rialto. Jews, marked by red hats, were being thrown over into the canal. There was gratuitous nudity in the first five minutes, followed by the question of homosexuality, played to a sensual extreme in this production. Perhaps it wasn't too late to change to *Twelfth Night*? He let the film continue running as he went into the tiny kitchen in search of whisky and a glass.

He pondered Antonio's relationship with Bassanio, and wondered if Shakespeare intended us to consider a physical relationship? It was strange — in an age when sodomy was punishable by death — that such obvious emotional love had been in print. Those with a personal agenda vowed that Shakespeare was gay, citing the young man of the sonnets. Not for the first time Derek considered getting out of teaching, maybe doing a Master's; an image of himself sitting quietly in a library, reading all day, was as seductive as it was impractical. There was a knock on his front door. He thought it must be a colleague — Paul came by occasionally unannounced to share a bottle and a general grouse. He'd be expecting an apology for his earlier rudeness.

'Max! What are you doing here?'

Max stood in the small entrance hall, looking wretched.

'You know this is out of bounds.'

Derek was mindful of how stupid this was, as the boy had stayed with him in the vacation. But school rules applied in term time. Max didn't move and in the light from the hallway

Derek saw in the boy's face the panic that he had first seen in the pizza shop, and that rooted him to the spot.

'Well come in and sit down, now you are here. Would you like a coke or a squash?'

'I don't mind.'

Derek fetched a can of coke from the fridge, and handed it to the still standing Max and knew to wait. After a few minutes Max pulled the ring on the coke; it spurted and made a mess on the rug.

'Never mind that. What is it you've come about?'

'Shall I get a cloth?' Max's eyes were fixed on the stain of coke on the already stained rug. Derek fetched a cloth from the kitchen.

'Sorry, Sir.'

'Mr Baker please, not Sir at home.'

'I think Daniel should play Portia,' Max blurted out. Derek had no doubt that Daniel and his coterie had been pressurising him.

'Have you read the play, Max?'

'Yes S…'

'Would you like to read some of it to me, out loud? Some of Portia, I mean?'

'Now? I don't mind, I mean yes.'

Derek left Max in the sitting room and went through to his bedroom, on the pretext of finding a copy of the play. He phoned through to Colin Peacock, who was on prep duty.

'I've got Max Henderson with me, he called round for a book he left behind at half-term. He's not up to speed with the rules yet. Don't worry about him. I'll walk him back to the dorm.'

Back in the sitting room, he pulled two copies off the bookshelves. 'They were here all along.'

Derek opened the play at Portia's most famous speech to the court and Max began to read. 'The quality of mercy is not strained …' His voice was clear, unbroken and confident, nothing Derek would have recognised from the half-sentences prised out of him at half-term. '… it droppeth like the gentle rain from heaven …'

The words pouring from this young boy stirred Derek until he thought he might choke. He stopped breathing, and the words found direct access to his heart.

'We do pray for mercy, and that same prayer doth teach us all to render the deeds of mercy.'

He burst with a sob, an alien noise that brought Max to an abrupt silence. Tears were rolling down his face. He realised the boy had stopped.

'Are you all right, Mr Baker?'

'Yes, yes, go on.' Max read the last four lines, and stayed with his eyes on the page until Derek, back in control, said, 'You read that beautifully. Have you acted before?'

'No, Mr Baker.'

'You must play Portia. I'll move things around and give Daniel Launcelot Gobbo; he loves playing the fool.'

Max, at ease, now accepted the cocoa that Derek offered and they talked about 'mercy', about forgiving those who trespass against us. The boy was intelligent, literary, and an hour passed easily. Max said he didn't believe in forgiveness; he thought that possibly things could be forgotten in time, but not forgiven, not if someone had killed or taken someone, or something, you loved. Derek was touched that the boy seemed to trust him and thought it best not to ask about his childhood. He was after all still there, on a cusp, a no man's land where intelligence supersedes experience.

'But Portia says Shylock has got to forgive,' Derek said.

'But they took his daughter, and he doesn't forgive; they trick him, and if forgiveness was a real thing then Antonio and his crowd should have forgiven him instead of forcing him to become a Christian.'

'I suppose Shakespeare had to write according to the prevailing religion and prejudice of the time,' Derek said. 'When did you read this play, Max?'

'I don't remember, maybe last year.'

'Have you read other Shakespeare plays?'

'Yes, Sir.'

'Which ones?'

'Most of them,' Max said, not looking up as he flicked through the pages, reading odd lines and happy in this world.

Derek had not read 'most' of the plays. He cleaned his glasses and watched, fascinated by this boy, with his well-washed blond hair hiding his face as he read, and his delicate, almost girlish hands turning the pages.

'And *Venus and Adonis*, *The Rape of Lucrece* and *The Sonnets*?' asked Derek.

Max looked up and his eyes were full of delight, almost Derek could believe, playfulness.

'Yes Sir, sorry Sir, I mean Mr Baker.'

It was quarter to ten, and lights out at ten; they'd have to move quickly.

When they reached Max's house, Derek said, 'You must definitely play Portia, I'm looking forward to it.'

He walked slowly back to his flat. It was a cold night with a clear sky; there would probably be a frost. On such a night as this Christabel would have sent him out with fleece for some of the delicate plants she tended in the school garden. Ah well, that was someone else's job now.

The boys had gone and most of the teachers. Those who remained on site were busy packing for the last of the snow in the Alps, or the first sun in the Canaries. A creak on the stairs alarmed him, but it was only a plumber for the flat above, taking advantage of the vacation to fix the shower. Derek had nothing planned and a much longed-for break could easily turn into a nightmare. Max Henderson had filled the mid-term vacation. A driver had collected him two days ago. He would probably be in Argentina now, with his mother. Caring for the boy, like he'd cared for Chris, had dropped him into a familiar groove. He'd have to think of something.

He opened the door to her wardrobe. He touched the fabrics, grief-filled dresses, sorrowful skirts and empty trousers. All had familiar stories. So many shoes; her feet deformed by years of dance meant she struggled to find comfort. He closed the door quietly, as though not to disturb her peace. Tomorrow he resolved, first thing, he'd put them all in bin bags and take them down to the charity shop. Then there was the chest; it too was full of her. He lifted the lid: dance clothes, untouched for years. He replaced the plastic box he'd collected last week from the undertakers. That was another challenge.

On the high street, he met Monica. She was one of Chris's friends, part of the tennis set, and reading group. She was older than them, well into her fifties, a retired teacher whom Hudson employed part-time to take the dyslexic boys for extra reading. Nodding towards her, he pushed open the door of the Oxfam shop. She was still there when he came out for the second load.

'Hello Derek, gosh you've been having a clear out.'

'Yes, it's Chris's things.'

'Oh, I'm so sorry, I didn't realise.'

'No, don't be sorry, you couldn't have known.'

'You must be feeling terrible, and I just blurted out. I could have helped you.' Derek winced at the thought. Should he have offered Chris's clothes to her? She was twice Chris's size, or more. They wouldn't have fitted her, but maybe there were other friends? He couldn't bear the thought — best for them to go to strangers. 'Will you come round and let me make you coffee? I've been meaning to call you.'

Monica was not a favourite with Derek (in fact he had often made excuses not to be in her company) but he said he would call; she was after all a connection to Chris.

'That's very kind, Monica. I'll park in the square and be with you in ten minutes.'

Monica's chaotic kitchen did not surprise Derek. It was messy, disorganised; not even the sort of untidiness that indicated an interest in cooking, or gardening, or any domestic pursuit; just a jumble of magazines, dirty washing, clean washing, breakfast remains, dirty dishes, sacks of vegetables, garden implements. Cupboards with their doors removed revealed years of dusty, sticky preserves and sauces, packets half empty, left unfinished before another was opened. Chris had not been like that.

'Push those magazines away and sit down,' Monica said, 'I really must have a tidy up.'

So she was aware of her shortcomings, Derek thought.

She shifted more debris and placed a cafetière and two mugs on the table. 'Do you take sugar?'

'Just one.'

'Me too, though I shouldn't.'

She poured the coffee. 'It must have been a hard day for you today.'

She put her head on one side and looked up at him, questioning, above her glasses. Derek felt like a small boy in her one-to-one reading sessions.

'Well, it was time to do it.'

'Dear Derek, do you miss her dreadfully?' She hadn't changed her expression.

'Oh, you know, one keeps buggering on'.

She wouldn't let go of that sickly questioning expression.

'I feel I want to give you a cuddle.'

Derek froze as she came behind him and put her arms round his chest.

'I'm getting through it,' he said, rigid with repugnance. She must have felt it, as she changed tack.

'I miss her too. She was such a sparkler; she had us in fits at the reading group. We were only saying last night, you should join us, it would be company for you, I don't know why you didn't come along before, except Chris said you knew too much!'

Derek was noncommittal.

'And tennis won't be the same this year without her and Tony. He was devastated, still is, not as much as you must be of course.'

'Tony who?'

'Tony,' Monica said loudly, as though it was perfectly obvious. Derek looked blank.

'You know Tony Belcher, Chris's doubles partner — used to be — sorry.' Derek still looked blank. 'He runs the sports equipment shop on South Street. You know him, don't you?'

'Yes, yes, just hadn't heard his name in a while.'

'Well I suppose he was Chris's friend.'

Was this woman implying something? Was she testing him? Derek changed the subject, asked about her children, holidays and other safe subjects and as soon as was polite said he had to go.

'You must call in whenever you want to, I'll organise a supper party for some of the tennis crowd, you must come along, I'll get Tony to come. Get you two together. I'll phone you.'

He left, but not as he had arrived, in simple sadness, but with a suspicion, a soft growth in the dark, refusing to be ignored.

Back in the flat, the door of the now empty wardrobe was open. 'Fuck, fucking fuck.' He slammed it shut. The coat hangers clanged with the force of the door closing. 'Fuck!' he shouted confrontationally at the Tupperware box. Next to the box was a pile of her journals. There were about a dozen; she'd been keeping them since before they met, two to three years per journal. They were neat and in order, 1989 to 2013; he chose 2011 and 2013, and carried them into the sitting room.

He opened the first book at April, the start of tennis. Yes, he was there. Why not? There was no reason why Chris shouldn't have a male partner. He flicked through to September. Tennis was on Tuesdays, his day for prep and dormitory duty. He usually got home around ten o'clock.

Tuesday 26th September. Living in a nightmare. Should I tell people? Who should I tell? Dear Derek is so loving it hurts. Tennis as usual, but not as usual, nothing is usual any more. Afterwards Tony and I drove out to the Golden Partridge; that was usual. I hadn't decided whether to tell him or not when I found myself saying that it was over between us. I hadn't planned to say this but as I was saying it I knew that it was right. He couldn't believe it, wouldn't accept it, said I was just a bit down, not feeling very well, time of the month, but it would pass. Now I wouldn't tell him. In the end he was abusive, said I had used him, which I suppose I had. I told him that I loved Derek and didn't want to deceive him any more. He said if Derek was such a great husband, why didn't he fuck me then? Foul, foul, foul. I'm glad it's over, I've been so stupid.

Derek stared through the window; the groundsman had been on the playing field, first mow of the season. A thrush was busy searching for worms to feed its babies. The beds Chris tended were full of weeds. At some point, she must have known he would read this. Damn her. She must have been very angry with him, like he was angry now. Before the illness they had had some spiteful rows. Sex had stopped; she'd wanted them to go to couples therapy. He'd been too frightened. There was stuff he didn't want ferreting out.

The thrush flew away suddenly; there was loud calling in the hedge and a magpie circled just above. He opened the second journal at the last entry.

13th September. Hospital tomorrow, or should I say last Chance Saloon? 'Hairless in Gaza' 'Christ stops at … The University hospital.' I AM SO FUCKING FRIGHTENED. Derek, my darling, I don't know if you will read this. If I come home I think I will burn all my journals. If you do read it, you will probably have read that I had a fling a while back. Please forgive me and think nothing of it. It was a silly time and a horrible mistake and I never stopped loving you. Today I can't stop thinking about our honeymoon. Do you remember we picked up every bit of confetti in the sleeper car because we didn't want the ticket inspector to know we were newly-weds? Take me back there darling, to the Hebrides. If you can't remember where we went, it's all written down. They always give you the ashes and then people don't know what to do with them. My mum put Dad in the garage because she didn't know what to do with him. Take me to Harris, to the beach at Scarista. Leave me where we began, like the poem. And don't be sad.

He landed on the beach on the island of Barra three days later. It was cold, grey and drizzling. He struggled into his waterproof trousers inside the terminal building—a wooden structure, a bit like an oversized beach hut. A few stragglers were drinking tea served through a hatch. His bike, booked online, was waiting for him, with the cycle shop owner outside.

'Are you going far, mate? If you're going north, you'll have the wind against you.'

'This wasn't my suggestion,' Derek said, as he transferred his luggage to the bicycle panniers. 'It was my wife's idea, this holiday.'

The owner looked at him questioningly. 'I've only brought the one bike.'

'No, no, this is fine,' Derek said, as he put the carefully wrapped Tupperware box, and red leather-bound journal, amongst his socks and spare trousers in one of the panniers.

'Off you go then. Enjoy your stay.'

'We will.' Derek rode off into the wind and the drizzle, with a wave. And so he swung between gung-ho and gloom. The man had been right about the wind. He forced the pedals painfully round, and twice in the first five minutes, a gust stopped him completely. His plan to cycle one and a half miles north to find the twelfth-century church of Cille Bharra seemed impossible. That June day with Chris, the sun had shone and they had walked to the church; now it was impossible even to imagine those conditions. It was all part of the dream that he had lost. Reaching a small incline, hardly a hill, he could not move forward an inch; holding the bike at a standstill was a challenge. A couple of cars passed, increasing his drenched condition; a third pulled up alongside.

'Can I gie you a lift?'

Derek shouted a polite refusal against the wind.

'You'll nae get there in these conditions. Best tae leave it till the morn — it's gang tae be fair.' The driver directed him back the way he had come and recommended a guesthouse in Northbay. 'You'll be all right riding south. You'll be there before you've started.'

Hospitality had not changed in twenty years of absence. The houses just seemed to be randomly placed here and there, with little relation to each other or any access road. He found 'Gaothach' as directed. It was a newly built house on the edge of Northbay. Aila introduced herself. She spoke in the soft island dialect, which defied the roar around her home, and undermined her brisk practical manner.

'Neil told me tae expect ye. Ah've a room at the back, it's a wee bit mair sheltered. Ah'll show ye. Ye can leave your bike in the shed.'

That he was expected confused Derek until later, when he met Neil, her husband, and recognised the man who had stopped his car. He wondered fancifully if Neil had been driving around the island looking for customers.

'The wind'll drop later, so it'll be quiet for ye to sleep. We don't really do evening meals but, as ye're on yur own, ye're welcome to come and join us.'

Derek, who couldn't contemplate setting off in search of a hotel or pub, accepted and sat down to sausage casserole with mash and cabbage with true willingness.

True to the forecast, the next day was bright. There was a blustery wind, east to west, which sent clouds rushing across the sky as though late for some heavenly convention. Neil offered to drive him to Cille Bharra but Derek preferred to give the bike a go, though he said he'd return to spend another night.

In the journal he read that they had picnicked there. He could see two chapels from the road — one roofless with broken walls, the other standing bravely against the elements. He cycled towards them, up the lane and through the empty car parking area. Balancing his bike with its pannier load against a low wall, he went inside the first building, where he became fascinated by the medieval carved grave slabs. He paused to read each one: a child dead at only a week old; it's mother in childbirth; three young men in war; other lovers lost, forgotten now; memorials only for the curiosity of strangers.

The second chapel was derelict, roofless. Within its walls, the screech of seabirds was amplified and aggressive — mostly Arctic terns, ferocious protectors of their young. Leaving his bike in the graveyard outside, he braved these angry attackers, and set off on foot up the hill to Ben Eoligarry. The wind that had tried to unseat him earlier had dropped and, despite being a hundred metres or more above sea level, it was calm. Yesterday's rain had made the primrose-covered ground greasy and he kept slipping. From the top, he could see across the Sound of Barra to Fuideigh Island, dotted with the white backs of rugged island sheep.

He chose a different route down, where he'd be less likely to fall. He came to Cille from behind. He couldn't see his bike; it wasn't leaning against the wall of the crumbling chapel where he thought he'd left it. Perhaps he'd been mistaken. He circled both buildings, checked inside and outside the perimeter wall. He had a small backpack but his lunch and Chris's ashes, side by side in their Tupperware containers, were in the panniers. There was no one to be seen; a minibus passed him on the road. There was nothing for it but to walk back. Every step brought conflicting emotions: anger at Chris for suggesting this holiday; then, realising the foolishness of the thought, anger at himself. Embarrassment at what he'd done — he'd not been careful, he'd failed to take proper care of her — numbing familiar guilt.

His walk back to Northbay took him past the airport. The café was just opening to welcome the daily flight. He ordered a cup of tea and a cheese roll from the woman behind the hatch

'You'll be on holiday then? I saw you come in yesterday. Hae you bin tae these parts before?'

Derek said that he had once before, twenty-four years ago. And that he'd just had his bike stolen.

'Och, are you sure now?'

Of course he was bloody sure, he felt like saying.

'There's nae much crime on the island, but you cannae be certain when the holidaymakers come.'

Derek did not like the tenor of the conversation and moved to a table.

She brought his cheese roll over and said, 'There's a part-time polis man on the island. You'll find him down at Castlebay. The number's on the notice board over there.'

Derek thanked her. He'd have to report it, or the cycle shop would make him pay. He took the number. When he called it later, there was only a recorded message. He spent the rest of the day tramping, climbing, aimless and miserable.

Neil and Aila were genuinely distressed at the theft of his bike, and offered all sorts of help, stressing the rarity of crime in the area. After supper—the remains of the casserole—an island whisky was produced, and Derek went to bed feeling less guilty. He'd done what she wanted and brought her to the island after all. Later, in a comfortable bed, fed, warm, inebriated, isolated and a stranger, his stranger wife came to him in the dark, accusing him; and later still he tramped the beaches in bare feet whilst her remains, scattered there, cut his feet, and the wind that blew from the north contained bits of her that made his eyes stream.

At breakfast, there was still no news of his bike. There was a couple having breakfast in the homely dining room of the guesthouse. And Derek, well mannered, told them his situation. They were sympathetic and wanted to help. They were exploring by car, they said, as you couldn't trust the weather, so they offered to run him to the cycle hire place where he had to complete some forms needed for insurance. From there he would easily be able to walk to the ferry and cross to Eriskay to continue his journey northwards. He had decided to hike.

Once the mist cleared, it was a bright cool day with sunshine. Spring flowers covered the fields and banks, the first lambs were out exploring, passing strangers beamed at him as if he was a newly-wed and this his honeymoon. They didn't know he'd lost his wife — again. He dealt with the business at the cycle shop and retraced his steps from the previous day, hoping that his luggage had perhaps been thrown aside by a felon who just fancied the bike.

The graveyard was uninhabited, as before. This would have been a good place for her to rest; she should have lain here. From Ben Eoligarry he could now see across the Sound. The terns screeched their accusations; and oystercatchers and curlews, busy foreigners, uncomprehending, fished and foraged below, amongst the rocks of Traigh Mhor. Towards the far end of the bay, a straggling group of walkers was approaching the beach from the north side, as he slid towards them from the south. Carrying kayaks on their heads, they made an outlandish party. The frontrunners were on the beach but half a dozen more were still way behind. Whoops and curses mingled with the seabirds' cries. Derek waited and watched from his end of the beach.

They were mostly boys, teenagers. A man seemed to be in charge and the boys set down their loads and erected windbreaks in response to orders. Gradually the whole group was beached and a second leader emerged, who had been encouraging from the rear. The boys were unruly; sudden fights would break out, stone throwing, sand kicking, cursing each other and whining their innocence to the adults. Smoke emerged from behind the windbreaks and most of the group gathered around it. As Derek reached halfway across the sand he could smell the wood smoke and bacon, reminding him of camping holidays when he was a boy. He called as he approached. Hearing him, some boys gathered aggressively in a gang, defending their territory as fiercely as the gulls. One of the two leaders emerged from behind the fire. Passing a sausage on the end of a stick to his fellow, he came to meet Derek.

'It's a wee bit better weather we're having today.'

'We can certainly do with it,' Derek responded.

'If you're on your own would you like to join us for a bite? I'm Kenneth by the way, and this rabble are a group of lads fae Glasgae.'

He was a broad man of about forty-five. Well-muscled, he stood with his back to the fire. The wind blew smoke across them both and they moved to prevent their eyes smarting, as some sparks shot out. Kenneth rubbed his hand across his balding head; what he lacked in hair had gone to make up a prize-winning pair of ginger eyebrows.

'That's Hugh playing football.' He indicated his compatriot playing further down the beach. Hugh was younger, taller, than Kenneth; late twenties, black hair, and executing some pretty nifty moves. Most of the boys were involved in the game, but there didn't appear to be teams — more like every man for himself. Derek said he'd have a cup of tea if there were one going. 'Aye, we've a flask of coffee. Come and join us.'

'Difficult kids, exclusions, violent families, never been out of the city, an rough parts at that.' Kenneth said that he and Hugh ran the club, paid for by the council and some private partnership.

'School holidays, we needed to get them away, gie them an experience.' Two boys nearby were shouting abuse at one another. Kenneth separated them and told the older boy to go and check on the barbecue.

'Fuck you!' the other boy yelled, as he returned to the game.

'Coffee coming up.' He and Derek sat on the sand.

'What d'you do?'

Derek said he was an English teacher down south. The game finished and Derek sat to the side as the boys jostled and joked with Hugh and Ken, fighting to be first for grub. Bacon buns in hand, they found groups to join. A boy yelled.

'Hiy Ken, there's sand in ma sandwich … joke … d'ye git it?'

Derek watched. They were just boys, not so very different from his lot. He finished his coffee and said he would be on his way.

'Why don't you stay with us? You're used to lads, and we could use another pair of hands.' Kenneth was magnetic; his eyes under those brows penetrated. Derek found himself compelled.

'Yes, sure, if I could be of help.'

'Right boys, this is Derek, he's an absolute wizard at kayaking and he's here to help. OK. Life-jackets on.'

There was a rush towards a pile of jackets, fighting and pushing, reasonably good-natured.

'Not quite a wizard Ken,' Derek said.

'Hae you done it before?'

'Once.'

'Och, like I said, you're a wizard.'

The boys were divided into groups: five first-timers with Hugh; four second-timers with Ken; and three younger, better-behaved boys with Derek. The boys raced, challenging the waves and each other. Derek kept seaward of his three, in case they set off for North America. An hour exhausted them and Ken was experienced enough to call them back before trouble. Back on land 'his' group demanded his attention:

'Whoar d'ye come frae?'
'Ur ye a fuckin' teacher?'
'Ur ye a virgin?''
'Ur ye married?'
'How auld ur ye?
'Rangers or Celtic, or a Harry hoofter English club?''
'England's shite — English are wankers.'

And they strutted about, speaking in mock-English accents with little fingers in the air, accompanied by much farting.

Ken and Hugh gathered them in, and got them organised after a fashion. Their tiredness calmed them.

Despite verbal complaints, the boys followed orders for the packing up. Derek was now involved and his gang of three stuffed life jackets into the kayaks. When they finished their task, Ken sent them to the sea to scrub the barbecue with water and sand and pack it in plastic.

'Ye on holiday, Sir?'
'Yep. And my name's Derek.'
'Oooo — Der-rick, bit ova prick.'
'That's enough now.'
'Yeh Billy, ye're the prick.'
'Billy the dick, big swinging dick, if ye look glum he'll shove it up yur bum.'

A fight was about to break out and, in stepping between them to break it up, as he'd seen Ken do, Derek took a thump in the chest and ended up in the waves.

'Sorry Sir, sorry Sir, you aw right? Gie me yur arm.'

They pulled him up, dripping but unhurt. They were genuinely sorry, and were quiet as they tramped back to the main gang.

'What happened to you?' Ken asked.

'I tripped and fell in.'

Ken's eyebrows questioned, but he said nothing.

'Don't stand there gawping — get the man a towel.'

Billy, Mark and Wesley, now initiation had been passed, were firmly his gang, rushed for towels and were enthusiastic in rubbing him dry.

The convoy set off over the headland to where the Boys' Club van was parked. Derek was carrying his share, Billy (whose fist it was that had taken the wind out of Derek and landed him in the surge) was by his side. Ken fell in beside them.

'We're camping on Eriskay. If you're going our way, will you join us for the night? We've a spare tent and we're putting a pig on a spit.'

'Och Derek, that wid be great!' Billy ran ahead, calling in his best English voice, 'Derek is joining us fur dinner, hae yi goat yir monkey suits and silver sairvice?'

'He's got your number,' Ken said.

Billy was a scraggy, undernourished boy, who looked younger than his fourteen years. He had greasy lank hair and pimples. His jeans hung so low they bagged around his knees so that he had to run wide legged from the hips to keep them on. Yet despite his physical appearance, when his rage was constrained, he sparkled like sun on the waves.

'Will you tell me about Billy?' Derek asked.

'It's the usual story,' Ken said. 'Single parent, hopeless alcoholic, probably other things as well. He was born addicted, which is probably why he's so scrawny. A fighter though. His dad was featherweight champion of Scotland before the drugs got him. So he says. Mebbe he made it up. He's been back and forward between his mum and foster parents all his life. If we can keep him clean, he might make it off the shit heap. He's a bright lad, good at figures.'

Derek sat up at the front of the van between Ken and Hugh. In the queue for the ferry the boys in the back kept up a deafening racket. It was a relief when the *Loch Alainn* let down the gate ready for boarding. A forty-minute crossing might be challenging with this cargo. Ken spoke quietly to them before he let them loose. Naturally they headed for the top deck and freedom from authority. The day was still fine and the ferry wasn't full. Derek stayed below, sharing a beer with his two new friends. Ken loved cars. The time he had free from work or the lads, which wasn't a lot, he would spend tinkering with his latest old wreck. He had grown-up daughters but had lost his wife to cancer five years previously. Hugh told of a fiancée who grumbled about the time he spent at the club.

'She'll hae you under her thumb in no time,' Ken joked. Two of the lads, rushed into the bar.

'Ken. Sir, Billy's throwin' up, they're haudin him ower the side.'

Hugh shot up, and Derek and Ken followed. When they got there, Billy had indeed been sick but was on a bench with everyone crowded round him. In the face of this minor event, the boys were as sympathetic and concerned as if his sickness were terminal. They'd fetched water, several cups full, and a jacket had been donated and put around his bony shoulders.

'Ah ye aw right noo, Billy?'

'Kin ah git ye anythin?'

'Here's Ken now, ye'll be OK'

'Is he OK, Ken?'

Billy was fine. His helpers were soon bored and more interested in leaning over the rail as their destination drew closer.

Derek had been drawn into this unfamiliar world and friendship had been bartered for some small, unnecessary assistance. If, like the boys, Ken and Hugh had made assumptions, they did not let it show.

At the campsite someone gave Derek a tent, a slightly mildewed sleeping bag and a ground sheet; he erected the former, got inside and — due to the effects of the exercise and the beer — fell asleep. He woke in the dark to a terrifying chant: 'kill the pig, kill the pig'. He became aware of rushing bodies close to his tent and, through the flap, flames and sparks. Then a bald head appeared through the flap, with eyebrows looking like fuzzy red caterpillars on a cliff ledge:

'D'ye fancy a beer?''

'Sure, I'll be out in a minute.'

'Dinnae mind the boys. We read *Lord of the Flies* with them over several weeks — they loved it.' Crumpled and a little stiff, Derek crawled out of his tent, uncurled himself like a child's Action Man that had been abandoned in the garden for too long, and found that Hugh and some helpers were lifting half a pig onto a spit.

'They can be kids again here. Well, I say again — most of them never had a childhood. If they're a bit infantile, that's OK by us.'

'Did you train for this work, Ken?'

'Noo, are you serious? It's common sense.'

The pig crackled. The chant was intermittent. The night was dry. Staring into the night away from the flames, Derek was thrilled by the massive sky adorned with a million stars. Beyond the reach of the fire it was quite cold, and with the sky so clear there would be a frost. The smell of roasting pork filled the air. Every so often, lads would pass and the smell of the crackling would be mixed with a waft of marijuana.

'As long as it's only a wee bit of pot, we turn a blind eye. If we find anything else, they're out. They know the score.'

The few other campers on the site turned up to the feast, bringing their own booze. Everyone crowded round for buns overflowing with moist tender pork and crackling.

'There's a local butcher gives us this every year.'

Derek ate and drank and chatted. It had been a long while (if ever) since he'd enjoyed such an evening. Later the boys moseyed off to their tents, and the other campers bid goodnight. Derek and Hugh sat by the glowing fire, and Derek felt comfortable and able to tell them about his loss; about his middle-class childhood and university education; his love of poetry; about meeting his wife when he was at university in South East London, reading for his doctorate, and she was across the road at the Laban Centre training to be a dancer; how her first job had been a world tour and how he'd followed her. Stalking, they might call it, except she didn't mind.

'Hey, I've got an awfy bad back — could you give me some advice?' Hugh asked, in earnest.

'Not that kind of doctor, ye pillock.' Ken respected education above all.

'There's *my* youth,' Hugh said, and kicked the ashes.

For Hugh, the world Derek described was far distant. A practical man, he'd not progressed beyond standard grades. The fire was dead, the night cold but they were reluctant to lose each other's company. Finally, Hugh said, 'Come back to ours for a nightcap.'

Their tent was luxurious. A four-person affair, they each had a separate sleeping space, and between the two there was a low table with bean bags and cushions around it. A bottle of whisky appeared, and Hugh produced a packet of large Rizlas and started to roll a joint. Derek accepted a pull as it was passed to him and Ken poured him a whisky; not the clear barley sugar liquid of the home counties pub, but something the colour of peat, smelling of moss and damp places, of wood smoke and old barns, of tea and citrus. Derek sipped, and accepted occasional pulls on the joint.

'All my organs are glowing. Can you see them?' Derek offered in surprise.

'Yeah, man.'

'Really, they are changing colour like an LED display. Wow, that's some whisky!' There was a pause before Hugh said, 'It might not be the whisky.'

Suddenly they were all three laughing. Derek went outside for a pee. He swayed back and forth, delighting in the splash on stone and mud, as if he had never heard that noise before. Hugh joined him on the other side of the tent opening. It was a duet. Derek looked up as he closed his flies, 'Wow!'

'What is it, man? What have ye seen?'

'What is the stars?'

'You tell me, you're the educated one. Come in now before you get too cauld.'

Inside Derek had another sip of whisky and another pull on a joint.

'My wife organised this trip.'

'I thought you told us she was…'

'Yeah…I mean she told me to come.'

'O…kay.'

'She came with me…only…I've lost her.'

'You OK man?' asked Ken.

'Yeah, her ashes. I brought her ashes, but they got nicked, with the bike.'

Hugh and Ken exchanged glances.

'So she's gone twice, it's very sad.' Derek looked like a little boy about to cry. Ken nodded and Hugh got up and went to his sleeping quarters. They could hear him rummaging. He emerged though the flap and held out the Tupperware box.

'Is this her?'

'Yes, that's her, that's my wife, how did you get her?'

'It was with a few of the lads last night,' Ken said, 'They must have nicked your bike yesterday afternoon when we weren't looking.'

'What were they doing with her?'

Derek took the box and held it to his chest.

'They were…attempting to snort her.'

There was a limitless silence in which Derek gently rocked his wife back and forth like a babe in arms, and the two Scottish men looked on in sympathy and awe. Finally, Derek made a noise. It was a chuckle, definitely a chuckle. Hugh giggled; there was a noise from Ken, decidedly a chortle; and then they swayed with laughter, clasped each other and hugged, still laughing. Then Derek, holding onto his box with fervour, thanked them for a lovely evening, as he would have done the headmaster's wife, and headed for his tent.

Max waited nervously at arrivals, looking for his mother. Suddenly she was there, as cool as the Northern Lights, among the short, dark, vibrantly dressed South Americans. She waved furiously.

'Darling, lovely to see you. How was the flight? Now where's Toby?'

Melly stepped into the road. Vehicles swerved, abuse or appreciation was shouted through car windows. A large black, tractor-like car pulled up, the driver's window slid down and a tanned hairy hand came through the window.

'Hiya Maxy, sling your bag in the trunk and get in.'

The boot opened, and Max did as he was told.

The car slid out into the traffic stream and Max silently watched as the shanties at the edge of the city turned into solid buildings and twenty-first century skyscrapers. Melly leaned over her seat.

'A little shopping first, get you kitted out.'

He stared at himself in the fitting-room mirror, grey and crumpled after his thirteen-hour flight, as his mother passed in armfuls of clothes.

'Darling, get undressed.'

Their eyes met, identical, pale blue. It had been two years since they had last been together and he had grown more like her. His hair unmistakably hers, facial bones hers. Not quite her height yet. As the clothes transformed him, the echo was all her. A soft leather jacket hung from his slim shoulders, trousers suspended from prominent hip bones. Assistants and shoppers paused, fascinated by the double beauty of mother and son.

They met Toby in a club frequented by Polo players. Toby ordered steaks in the bar. 'Argentinian beef. Best in the world eh, Mel?'

A piece of meat that completely covered a dinner plate was placed before Max. He struggled to eat it but two-thirds was left on his plate at the end of the meal.

'Don't worry, my friend. After a week on the farm you'll be eating like a gaucho. You excited?'

'Er yeah.'

'A man of few words, eh? Don't you worry, just talk to your horse, that's all you need to do.'

He placed his hands on Max's shoulders and steered him through the crowded bar.

The car was comfortable and air-conditioned; the scenery flat unchanging grassland, burnt brown by the hot summer's final fling. Max was asleep when they arrived three hours later at the long, L-shaped, low ranch building. He was shown to his bedroom and told to 'freshen up'. Beyond the lace curtains and the open window, it was early evening and the sun was still warm. Wind gusted through the yard. A door to a loose box, fastened on a longish chain, rattled and banged and collections of dust and straw made sudden dashes for freedom, only to be toyed with by the wind and caught again in corners. He responded to his mother's calling and joined her and Toby on a verandah at the front of the property. Melly swung gently to and fro, on a hammock, pushing herself by one slim foot with bright varnished toenails. She sipped from a cocktail glass.

'A beer for the boy!' Toby called to a young man in an apron who was standing nearby.

Max tasted his beer and paid little attention to his mother and Toby discussing plans, though he was vaguely aware that some of them included him. He looked across the garden: a mowed lawn, sprinkled to lushness; shrubs he did not recognise; and from time to time a turkey would strut by, searching for delicacies.

Supper was served by Carmen, a middle-aged woman with dyed blonde hair caught in a ponytail. She brought steak and beans and salad and vegetables, and to Max's relief placed a pizza in front of him. There was wine, which he did not drink, and more beer, which he did not drink. Carmen brought him a coke. After dinner Tobias and his mother sat on the verandah smoking and drinking coffee while Max sat indoors, in front of a mile-long television, trying to understand what was being said. Bored but not tired, he switched the TV off and concentrated on learning his lines for *The Merchant of Venice*.

He woke early. From the previously deserted yard came a cacophony of sounds: studded boots on stone, a crowing cock, human shouts, stable doors banging, horse-shoes on concrete, conversations, two speakers, three speakers, a small car engine, the deeper growl of a tractor, a bell clanging, yard tap gushing, incomprehensible calls: 'desayuno amigo', 'wii rapido'.

In the kitchen now, the table was full — twelve, fourteen people, mostly men. Chairs scraped as the occupants rose to refill plates. People touched him, on his shoulder, his back, his arm — a seat was pulled out for him, plates pushed towards him, scrambled eggs, omelettes, bacon, cheese, spicy sausage, beefsteak. At the head of the table Tobias beamed.

'Welcome my friend, OK.'

He banged the table for silence.

'My stepson Maxy, here from England for three weeks to have good time and learn to ride. They send us a school boy, we send them back a gaucho!'

Shouted greetings and table banging welcome all round.

'Now help yourself, a good breakfast will keep you going.'

Max, feeling overwhelmed and fighting panic, ate scrambled eggs he did not want. Gradually the table cleared as the workers cleared their plates and went out to the yard. Tobias pulled up a chair next to Max. He indicated an older gaucho across the table.

'Enzo here will look after you, we have a bonito pony for you.'

'Si, si,' the man said, with grease running down his chin. He gave an open-mouthed grin and Max could see the half-chewed bacon in amongst a few teeth. Tobias turned and discussed work matters in Spanish with groups of his workers. Max gazed at him, fascinated; other men in his life, masters at his school, his father and his cronies were not like this picture book hero. Black curly hair, powerful muscles defined through his T-shirt, he was tanned like polished wood; there was music in his voice as he switched languages.

He turned to Max. 'You want more?'

'No thank you.'

'Good boy, Enzo will show you the pony.'

Max followed the small man in a dirty poncho, out of the kitchen and across the yard. The man limped and spoke constantly but whether to Max or to himself was unclear; if to Max, he was not understood. In a tack room he took a pair of chaps and offered them to Max, who had no idea what to do with them. Enzo stooped to wrap them round his calves. Max jumped back at the touch and completed the task himself. Enzo then led him to a loose box where a chestnut pony was already saddled. Now his prattle was directed at the horse. He blew in its nostrils and kissed its nose, breaking off occasionally to spit through a gap in his teeth. He exchanged the pony's halter for a bridle and led him out to what Max later learned was the training corral.

'OK, hasta abora.'

Max, terrified, understood. Enzo guided Max's left hand to the horse's mane, and his right foot to a stirrup. The horse danced forward and backward. Max — hopping on his left foot — tried to stay with him, but failed and landed flat on his back on the soft ground, looking up at Enzo, who was wheezing with laughter beside a perfectly still pony. He got up. His new jeans were dusty and his chaps had swung round. He tried to brush himself clean. Relived that no one had witnessed his fall, he re-buckled his chaps and tried again. This time Enzo grabbed his foot as he lifted it towards the stirrup and, as if by magic, Max found himself in the deep saddle, clinging to the front of it.

Enzo stood in the middle of the corral with the chestnut pony on a long rein and shouted instructions. Max was in the saddle, trusting his grip like a sinner does his prayers, whilst the pony dutifully trotted round the perimeter of the circle. Enzo stopped the pony to gather the reins back into Max's hands but moments later they were loose round the pony's legs. During the nightmare, young men and women, workers on the ranch who had gathered to watch, shouted encouragement or laughed.

Max's vision, disjointed by the pony's jerks, was like a cubist painting, through which he spotted Tobias. He let go of the saddle and tried harder to master his mount. Enzo shouted to the pony to increase its pace; something took its attention and it shied away from the fence and Max was again on the ground. Enzo, wheezing through his teeth, once more got Max aboard by grabbing his ankles. Tobias was no longer watching. Max hit the ground five more times, before the lesson was over and he was left to his own devices.

In the garden later, lying on his back, watching the fast-moving clouds, Max daydreamed he was on a black horse, galloping across the pampas, rounding up cattle and swinging a lasso, and then drinking beer with the gauchos after a hard day, and joking with Tobias. Each day he tried harder with his lesson and gradually he learnt to mount without assistance and let go his hold on the saddle. Apart from his riding lessons, he was mostly left to himself. He saw little of Tobias, only for a few moments at breakfast; and even less of his mother, who got up late and took the car to visit friends or go shopping. She did not watch his lessons but if they met at dinner she would ask how he was enjoying himself. There was to be a party, he learnt, in two weeks' time: families from nearby and friends from the city, an ox on the spit, live music and dance, and 'beautiful girls' Tobias said, winking at him. Tobias was drinking heavily; he'd been into town and lunched at the polo club.

'What sort of girls do you like, big breasts or big bottoms eh?'

Max felt his face go red.

'Leave him alone Toby, you've drunk too much.'

'OK…what about this fancy school of yours where you don't learn Spanish or how to play polo? Whaddya do there? Eh?'

'Toby, I'm warning you.'

'Nah, seriously,' Toby leaned forward, 'wash your favourite thing?'

'I like English.'

'But you speak English.'

'No, literature, plays and things.' Still blushing, and glancing at his mother, who was looking tense, he told them about *The Merchant of Venice*, and having been chosen above lots of others to play one of the leading roles.

'Darling that's marvellous.'

'Can you come?'

'Maybe, when is it?'

'Wash this part you've got?' Tobias reached for the whisky bottle.

'Portia.' Melly winced.

'Who's he?'

'It's a woman, she dresses as a man and pretends to be a lawyer and stops Antonio being killed.'

'A woman!' He bellowed and spilt whisky on the table.

'It's an all-boys' school, Toby.'

'Yeah, and they chose the patsy to play the girl.'

Melly leaned over and slapped Tobias hard across the face.

'Go up to bed, Max. It's just because he's drunk. He picks on people — he doesn't mean it.'

Tobias staggered to his feet.

'Go now, I can handle it.'

From upstairs Max could hear his mother screaming, and Toby roaring. Crockery was smashed and furniture thrown. It stopped abruptly with a door slam. Max went to the window and saw the black car swerve up the drive towards the highway. He watched till it was out of sight, then he crept downstairs. He heard his mother crying in the kitchen. He waited for her to stop before going back up. He opened his wardrobe ('closet' his mother called it), threw all his new clothes on the floor and got inside, pulling the door closed.

Max did not go to breakfast the next morning. Muffled and shrunken in his shell, he heard Enzo's cracked and distant voice calling him from the yard. Later his mother opened the door. She talked brightly, like a steel pin cracking through his carapace. Did he want to drive into town? See an American movie? Max did not answer or move and she went away. No one else came. In the early hours of the next morning he slid silently through the dark building, and fed himself from the giant refrigerator.

In the days that followed he got up late and had breakfast leftovers when the men had gone to work. Carmen came to expect him; there was always a box of food waiting. He read in the garden. Mostly poetry. He read the poems of Pablo Neruda. He read from morning till night and lived in detail what he had read. In the afternoons he explored the creek, taking his clothes off and bathing when it was deep enough. Sometimes he would sit on a stone in the middle of the flowing stream and just think; he made up stories and poems, but never writing them down he did not know their worth.

Between him and his day of departure loomed the end-of-season party, a grand annual affair after which the casual staff would head to the city for the winter. Melly pleaded with Max to come, and they struck a bargain. He would attend the party and she would come to *The Merchant of Venice*.

It was a dull start to the day, clouds were gathering in the east. Max lay in bed till he was sure the crowd had left the kitchen. He expected his usual late breakfast and fuss from Carmen but she was not there. The kitchen was scrubbed clean. He wandered through the living room and out onto the veranda overlooking the garden. Everywhere was activity: a bandstand had been erected and was in the process of being strung with brightly coloured paper flowers, electric cables lay strewn about, workmen on ladders were hanging lights in the trees, and loudspeakers on poles. The balustraded verandah was garlanded in ribbon and lace as though in expectation of a bride.

Beyond the yard and the garden was a wide strip of grassland that ran around the circumference of the Estancia. On this occasion every year it was mowed and marked up as a racetrack. In the stable yard a brick barbecue the size of a small house had been built, with a spit that would hold a beast. Horses and ponies were tethered nearby and girls were plaiting flowers in their manes and tails. Max recognised his chestnut pony. He had not been near him for two weeks. He went over and felt the pony's breath, warm and delicious and wondered, if the pony recognised him. The girls giggled as they twisted and combed. In the riding circle, fresh sand had been laid and Enzo was making it smooth with a large wooden rake.

'Hey, Maxy, where you been eh?'

So the sod speaks English, Max thought and waved at him.

'You gonna ride your pony arder de pardy?'

Max smiled and Enzo's familiar toothless wheeze followed him out into the orchard.

'You old bastard,' said Max under his breath.

Under the burdened apple trees, tables were being set up and Carmen was ordering her kitchen helpers to cover the tables with paper cloths and small bouquets.

'Max.' Carmen called him over and gave him a tray of candles set in glass jars to place on each table. He was pleased to have a task. The girls were in high spirits and called loudly to each other and laughed; he may have been the butt of their jokes but he didn't notice.

Finishing his job, he wandered back in the direction of the yard. He had a mission — to find a quiet, dark place, where he could disappear when his mother was engaged with her guests. The loose boxes were dark and smelt of sweet hay, but he could be sure of being left alone. The tack room offered better possibilities. It was a long room that ran behind the gauchos' stabling. He could hear them stamping behind the wall, disturbed at their change of routine. Along one long wall ran bank upon bank of saddles, opposite which were hanging bridles and tack of every description. At the end was a separate area where spare boots and chaps, brushes, ointments and lotions were stored; used once and left to the dust. He found a corner behind a box of brushes and squeezed in. From inside he could see the length of the tack shed and up above into the hay loft but he was invisible. He stayed for fifteen minutes until he felt secure enough to venture out again into the bright yard.

Whilst he had been inside, the sky had cleared and the sun shone low in the sky, squeezing its last warmth to celebrate the day

Guests began arriving at around one in the afternoon. Max perched on a fence, watching the procession of vehicles moving up the mile-long drive: workmen from neighbouring establishments in trucks, also festooned with paper flowers and streamers; young men on motorbikes, their girls on the back; gauchos on horseback; off-road vehicles; trailers full of girls; vans and caravans. It made quite a carnival. Drivers leant on their horns and challenged the music blasting from the speakers around the designated car park. From his spot on the fence he watched them spill out of their vehicles, shake dust from their clothes, adjust combs in their hair, call or wave to friends. They followed signs to the bar or barbecue, eager to sign up for games and competitions.

Max, separate as always, was drawn to the lunging circle where there was an electric bucking bronco, well managed by Enzo and now containing boys of Max's age who were queuing up to have a go. Most could not sustain more than thirty seconds. It was a pleasure for Max to see them all hit the ground, accompanied by Enzo's whistling chortle. Moving around the edge of the crowd, he heard his name called. Melly was waving at him from the verandah. She was at the centre of a small gathering, drinking champagne and watching the throng enjoying the festivities below. He made his way towards them.

'Maxy, darling, you must meet Mr and Mrs Ferguson.'

'Hi there, call us Col and Mary.' Max shook hands.

'And this is our son Joel and his sister Charlie.'

'Hi.'

'It's a grand spread you got out here. Now, why don't you young ones go and enjoy yourselves down there?'

'Sure thing, let's go,' said Joel.

Joel was fifteen and nearly two years older than Max; his sister was twelve. They were from Texas. Joel said they were in the process of selling up and buying an Estancia down here, they wanted more land to run a different sort of beef. The way he talked, it was as if the whole venture was his idea and his operation. 'How many steers you got on this outfit?' Max had to admit he had no idea and that he was here for the first time on holiday from boarding school in England. Joel continued his swanking, talking loudly about all he saw. He didn't think much of the ponies tethered in the yard — he called them 'horseflesh' — although he quite liked the little chestnut filly and thought he might give her a go later. Max hoped that his pony would get Joel in the dust as often as she had him.

'There's a bucking bronco in the corral. Do you fancy a go?' asked Max.

'Sure thing, lead on young fella.'

Max grimaced.

The queue had lessened. Joel asked if Max wanted to go first, but Max said Joel should because he was the guest. Max waited the nineteen seconds it took for Joel to land, arse in the dust, and — before Enzo had time to wheeze — he left the gathering and headed towards the barbecue.

He was hungry and remembered he'd had no breakfast. He grabbed a bun overflowing with roast beef and sat on a bench close to the tethered horses. Before he finished eating, some of the stable staff came and gathered up the horses. The sound system interrupted the music to make an announcement in English and Spanish about the races. Max recognised Toby's voice. Those who had signed up were invited to gather at the start line. Various groups began to move in the direction of the track. He heard Melly, and saw her across the yard. There was no escape.

'Maxy, we lost you — come and join us to watch the races.'

Melly and Tobias, with their new Texan friends, Col, Mary and their daughter Charlie, bore down on him.

'Why haven't you signed up to ride?' Melly asked. Didn't his mother know about his failure?

'Joel's riding, isn't he, Col?'

'Yeah, well he could ride a horse before he could walk.'

Max said nothing but reluctantly joined the party, who moved off towards the course. Tobias had a good place reserved on a bend near the finish line. There were rugs on the ground, shooting sticks for those who wanted them, and hampers with plastic champagne glasses and plenty to drink.

'Don't you ride?' asked Charlie.

'No.'

'Gosh! I have my own pony. We do dressage and show-jumping.'

Joel was not in the first race, which was a fun one for the little children who had to get up and down off their ponies, collecting plates. Then some of the gauchos did demonstration riding which involved lassoing. Max, to his mother's horror, sat on a rug and began reading. She came close.

'This isn't our bargain,' she whispered. Max felt obliged to watch as Joel came round the bend, way ahead of the field, on 'his' chestnut pony. The company screamed and cheered. As he approached the finish, he beat the pony furiously on its hindquarters.

'Why is he doing that? Stop it! He's won anyway.' But nobody was listening.

Joel joined them, sloughing off the congratulations. He perched on the rail of the racetrack, keeping his balance with one foot on the ground. Max looked across at the older boy from where he was sprawled on the rug. He saw denims tucked into maroon tooled and decorated cowboy boots, thick belt decorated like the boots round his slim waist, check open-necked shirt, dark hair; he'd be shaving soon. A group of girls stood on the bank above them.

'Eh Joel, you won the race!' one shouted.

'Better than Jarcovsky,' Joel shrugged.

'Wow!'

'Jarcovsky's my brother,' shouted another of the girls,

'You wanna meet him?'

Joel looked at his father.

'Sure, you go.' Col Ferguson beamed. 'Take young Maxy with you.'

Joel sprang from the rail and headed up the bank to be swathed by teenage girls. Max remained on the rug. After the party had headed back to the terrace, thankfully without paying him any attention, Max took a roundabout route to the tack room. Passing through the orchard, he caught a glimpse of Joel propped against an apple tree with three or four girls lounging at his feet.

He craved blankness. Squeezing himself into the corner he'd previously located, he pulled a horse blanket over his head. Now he just had to wait — wait for his skin to tranquillise, his lungs to smooth, his face to fall off, his joints to undo, his senses to stop. He was patient, time passed; after a while he would look for the vibration on his palms and soles that signalled his renewal.

All was quiet; all was dark. Senses coming back slowly, warm dung, sweet hay. There was a noise, rustling, too close. A muffled squeal. More rustling. He pulled back the corner of the horse blanket, his eyes adjusted to the dim light. He could see the length of the tack room, shafts of sunlight, swirling particles. Movement above, people in the hayloft. A couple, he knew why. He was trapped. A young man on his knees, his back to Max. Max knew who. Knew the belt that fell from loft to ground and jingled on the concrete. Tight denim lowered over muscled buttocks, hands caressing, thighs trembled. He saw her black hair, knew where her lips were, heard the boards creak as she lay back, saw the thrust, watched the throb, the push, the bottom — too beautiful — lift and descend. Touched himself. Came in unison. First time.

It was dark, fairy lights twinkling in the trees challenging the stars above. Max moved dreamily about the orchard, couples and families at tables talked and laughed quietly, no one noticed, noticed what? Max climbed the verandah steps.

'Max, we've missed you, where have you been?' Melly was speaking to him.

'I've been with Joel,' Max said slowly, purposefully.

Joel lifted his eyebrows, said nothing.

'Come and sit by me, darling. I've not seen enough of you.'

In the Outer Hebrides, Lewis to be exact, Derek was tramping the Pentland way, the old road from Breascleit village to Stornaway. Ten miles of solitude, just him and the brutal wind. Chris was still in her box. He had passed Scarista beach two days ago, but was put off by families, children playing, and noisy shouts; he hadn't wanted to leave her there with strangers. Now it was his last day. He left the road and hiked about three hundred yards across the plateau. At the edge of a small tarn he crouched behind a boulder to get some relief from the battering North-Easterly.

'Here, Chris?' he asked. The wind moaned '… I guess so,' he answered himself, 'it's not pretty, but neither is death. It is a powerful beauty; this landscape and the terrible angel will come with the eagles and kites. And all that is petty and all that belongs to the earth is gone now. I think this is what you wanted.'

Placing himself with his back to the gale, he opened the box.

'Off you go. We were joined once, I can keep you no longer…now we are separate.' He slipped back behind the boulder so that nothing of her should blow back on him.

'Now I too am free, but earthbound, to make the best of it I can.'

Closing the empty box and placing it back in his rucksack, he returned to the road; several hours later he deposited it in the first bin he came to in Stornaway.

Sixteen sat round a dark oak table. Heavy curtains framed the widows. Blinds covered the glass and obscured the view of the drive. They were invariably drawn to protect the inferior oil paintings of dead headmasters and landscapes that covered the walls. Table lamps directed light to the papers in front of the assembled staff. Derek was jolted back to the present by appreciative laughter at a *bon mot* from Hudson. He smiled automatically and speculated on where Hudson, might have spent his holidays? Hudson was younger than Derek. He was an ex-fitness instructor, ex-Royal Marine, ex-city broker and now a headmaster, married to an older woman who always seemed to be ill. He was inviting discussion on extra sport for the Summer Term and looking straight at Derek.

'Boxing?' Derek said.

He had been thinking about Billy and his boast about his dad being a featherweight champion of Scotland. He imagined Billy coping in this environment. He'd take on the likes of Daniel and his crowd. There were other suggestions from staff. Fencing? Horse riding? Golf had been dropped due to lack of interest. Hudson considered boxing.

'Last time we brought it in there were complaints from quite a few parents. We could try again,' he mused. 'Maybe in the winter? I wouldn't have thought boxing was your sort of sport, Derek.'

The meeting bored on, tea and biscuits were wheeled in by Mrs Hudson, and a break taken to enquire after her health. There were still five agenda items to go; Derek calculated this meant another two hours, at least.

'Thank you, my dear, now we'd best get on. We'll leave the new equipment for the science labs until last, as Mr Jacobs has promised to be here by five p.m. So the next item is the cricket pavilion. You will notice that the roof has been repaired over the holidays…'

Derek drifted back to his thoughts about Billy, imagining the reality TV show where Billy changed schools with Max …then on to his production of *The Merchant of Venice* with Billy playing Launcelot Gobbo, the jester, the badly fed and much put-upon servant of Shylock. And Max, among the gang on Barra, a strange beauty, collecting his shells, inviolable, like a sea anemone, resilient against the tide.

'What? Sorry.'

I was saying, Hudson repeated, 'last, but not least,' though clearly he thought it was, 'the arrangements for the end of year Shakespeare play.'

'Yes, of course, *Merchant of Venice*. The boys have their parts and hopefully will have learnt them during the vacation.'

'Well done, well done. Sure of your choice? Lot of Jewish boys in the school.'

'Rajahd is playing Shylock — he's from Saudi.'

Crossing the quad after the meeting, he saw Max pay the taxi and pick up his luggage, setting off for the dorm block. He looked in Derek's direction but did not acknowledge him.

Max was first back to the dorm. Olly and Sam, his roommates, were squeezing out the last of the hols with their loving families. He had grown, in the way that thirteen-year-olds could suddenly put on inches. New school clothes had been delivered, but there was no need for them until Monday. In a drawer under his bed was an orange Sainsbury's bag. Good, the cleaners had left them. He set off to the cricket pavilion, where he kept his collection in a disused locker. It was a shock, finding the changing room completely refurbished. The lockers no longer existed. He sat on the pavilion verandah, gripping the arms of his chair to stop the fragmentation — bits of himself speeding to the boundary, cracks like hard balls on willow exploded in his mind. Dennis, the groundsman, was heading for the wicket, pushing a roller. Max steadied, gripped tighter.

'Where are the lockers?'

'They've all gone, nobody used them anymore.'

'Where?'

'Grand old fire we had, there've been quite a few changes. The old potting shed, and the greenhouse, quite a conflagration.'

'I left something here.'

'No, it were all empty.' Dennis turned and continued with the roller.

The old potting shed, and the derelict greenhouse had been razed to the ground. In their place was a neatly paved area with benches and as yet unplanted borders. Max searched every inch before sitting on one of the shiny varnished benches. His stones, his shells, were part of the hard core that it sat upon. An inscription on the bench read:

'In Loving Memory of Christabel Baker,
Beloved wife of Derek. 1972-2014.'

Dr Hudson and his wife approached.
'Ah, Henderson, isn't it? Max?'
'Yes, Sir.'
'You've found our memorial garden.'
'Yes, Sir.'
'You with Mr Baker this term?'
'Yes, Sir.'
'In the school play?'
'Yes, Sir.'
'Who are you playing?'
'Portia, Sir.'
'Well done! Good hols?'
'Yes, Sir.'
Hudson took his wife's arm and wandered off. 'Strange boy,' he whispered in his wife's ear when they were out of range, 'that business of his father — never resolved.'

Derek was pinning a notice on the Drama Society board, calling a full-cast rehearsal of *The Merchant of Venice* on Thursday after school, when Hudson passed on his tour.

'Don't you use the intranet for that sort of thing? I'd like to get rid of all the notice boards. Untidy things.'

'I use both — it gives them less excuse.'

Through Derek's head flashed Billy, Mark, Wesley…

'Now calm down, this is the headmaster, Dr Hudson'

'What's that, Baker?'

'Oh sorry, nothing, Sir' He hadn't realised he'd spoken aloud.

'Take it easy, old man.'

The boys' voices continued in his head:

'Doctor? Whit ye doin' here? Ye got any Viagra? Wesley cannae keep it up, can ye Wes?'

'Where's yer tardis?'

'Where's the floozy?'

He imagined them racing down the corridor, singing the *Dr Who* theme tune.

Hudson broke the silence. 'Just met Max Henderson. Says he's your Portia. Hope you can get him to speak up. By the way, take a look at the old kitchen garden. We've made some improvements.'

Max was still on the bench when Derek came to look at the 'improvements'.

'Hello Max, you're back early.'

Max did not move or say anything. His pale blue eyes stared beyond Derek. He hardly appeared to be breathing.

'Mind if I sit down?'

Nothing. Derek stared at the clean white paving, at the empty earth of the beds, at the grey sky, and listened to distant sounds of cars on the gravel drive, to the shouted farewells. Minutes later (maybe five, maybe fifteen), Derek felt the body next to him soften. He left it a little while longer, then said, 'Good to see you, Max. Did you enjoy your holiday.'

'Yes, Sir.'

'What did you do?'

'I stayed on a ranch in Argentina with my mother and her boyfriend.'

'That must have been an experience. Have you thought of writing something about it?'

'Maybe. What did you do, Sir?'

'I went to the Outer Hebrides to scatter my late wife's ashes.'

'Will you write about that?'

'Probably.' And Max's face did something Derek had never seen before, from those cold distant eyes and anxious mouth. Max smiled.

'We could swap then,' he said.

'This Launcelot, does he gob a lot? Is he gobby? Works fur this Shylock, right. He's his laddie, an errand boy? Does his dirties? Fancies his lassie. Gies her one, eh?'

'No, I don't think so, Billy. Not the daughter bit anyhow.'

Derek engaged with his imaginary boys.

'Well, if you got some posh boy twat playing her Ah'm glad about tha.'

Wes joined in 'Antonio, reit, he's got a gang down the docks. Him and Shylock, rival bosses, struttin' with his pound of flesh. Shylock should have cut his tadger off, that wud a done it.'

Thursday afternoon, the boys were all there, chatting quietly in groups, waiting. Derek noticed Max, sitting just slightly apart from the others. He gathered them into a circle and began.

'We are going to set the play in Glasgow, in the 1940s, just after the Second World War. There was rationing then and that gave rise to a lively black market. Control of the docks was vital, and there were rival gangs. Antonio was Mr Big. Shylock ran a supply chain — anything, anywhere, no questions asked.'

The boys looked eager, excited even.

'Do we have to use Scottish accents, Sir?'

'Well Ian as Antonio, you are from Scotland so I reckon you could do a passable Glaswegian.'

'Och aye, Sir, I can do thaat.' This was received with much hilarity. The room resounded with 'hoots man' and 'och aye the noo' and 'where's yer troosers?'

'Daniel, you are a good mimic. Perhaps you could do Gobbo as a bit of a Glasgow yob.'

'Launcelot Yobbo,' someone said.

'The rest of you can use your own accents.'

'Is Antonio a poof, Sir?'

'If you mean, is he homosexual, gay, then I think the writing is ambiguous, and we cannot assume that the sexual mores of the Elizabethan period are the same as they are today.' Derek was pleased to have been handed this opening. He continued, 'There are many issues of race and religion, gender politics, feminism and homosexuality contained in this play; they will make for lively discussion in your citizenship class with Mrs Yates. Here we just explore the text and create a world for the play.' He made a mental note — must warn Susan Yates.

'OK, on your feet, we'll do a warm-up.'

Derek was quite pleased with his first rehearsal. Tomorrow would be soon enough to tell Paul that they'd have to paint over the Rialto and substitute a 1940s shipyard on the Tyne.

'Ah dinnae see why ye should get an award fer just goin on fuckin holiday.'

'It wisnae a holiday, we did stuff.'

'Oh yeah? Wha'?

'Anyways, Ken said I should invite yer.'

'Fookin Ken this and fookin Ken tha'! Wha' about doin' stuff fer yer auld ma? Get us a packet o' cigs and a tin o' stout, then mebbe I'll come.'

'No, youse won't.'

'Weel, go to the shop anyways.'

Ken had opened up the community room and then stepped outside to talk to Ivan, a resident who was bletherin' on about the club as usual.

'Youse need to keep control of those young lads. They're always clatterin' and droppin' their rubbish. They make this place a shite 'ole.'

'Aye, aye, but they're no bad lads,' Ken said, though he knew full well that they could be. He was twitchy. Tonight was important. He went to open the store next door to get the chairs out. Now he couldn't find where he had put his keys.

'What yer lost?' Ivan said.

'Keys'.

'Och, I'm always doing tha'. Mebbe they slipped oot yur pocket, doon tha drain.' Ken shook his head, but looked anyway.

A group of about five youths, his work party, came round the corner of the block. He watched them, judged their mood. They moved like a small pack of dogs, dominant or submissive, together yet separate, a couple split off to dribble a beer can. A young woman passed along the walkway of the opposite block and the lads responded with the obligatory jeers. They gathered where Ken was still searching. Uncommitted even as to which leg to stand on, they leaned, squatted, or sat on the low wall that delineated the cloistered entrances to the flats, from where they made forays to kick a piece of rubbish or throw a stone.

'Whit yur lookin' fer?'

'I've lost the fff-rigging keys.'

'Was that swearin', Ken?'

'Never mind, get off your arses and help me look.'

A couple of lads responded, kicking up a bit of dust. The road that ran past this end of the block ran round to the recycling yard. In a hot summer you had to keep your windows shut against the stink. Luckily, hot summers were rare.

'Whit's tha' hangin' in the door?' said the youth who was sitting on the rail. Ken swore under his breath.

'All right, clever clogs — ye can help me set up now.'

The community hall was on the ground floor of the flats and was well used: sewing classes (mostly Pakistani women), Pilates, Zumba, painting classes, adult literacy. A meeting space for complaints: the drains, the paper-thin walls, the damp, the draught, the leaking shower, the smell of gas. Some of them got attended to, only to return, and most not. Friday evenings, from seven to ten p.m, was boys' club for twelve to eighteen-year-olds. Not many kept coming beyond sixteen; by then, they could pass for eighteen and could do other stuff in the city.

Tonight Ken had someone coming from the Council to talk to the boys about the Youth Achievement Awards and to present the first awards won by his group.

Ken gave instructions — the gang put out the table for the dignitaries and chairs in rows for the audience.

'How many shall we put out, Ken?'

'Well, there are twenty of youse lot, and then there are your families.'

'Yur'll be lucky.'

'Haven't you got anyone coming, Mark? After all, you've got a silver.'

'Me da says he might come, as long as he can get to the boozer by nine.'

'We're running a bar here, cans of beer and wine for the ladies, you'll be surprised how many will turn up.'

'Ye dinnae tell us tha'?'

'It was on the letter, didn't you read it?'

'Can we have beer then?'

'Definitely not.'

By now people had begun to arrive, and the bar opened. Those of his lads who had arrived looked embarrassed to be with their mums and/or dads.

Ken was on the door, engaging the parents he hadn't met before, greeting those he had. He tried to keep a count of his lads. Seventeen he reckoned were in the hall, most with one and some with two parents, and the boys whose grandparents had come from Lithuania in the sixties had whole families with them. The room buzzed, it looked like a crowd.

He put his head out of the door to see if there were any latecomers. Billy was sitting on the wall.

'Are you waiting for someone, Bill?'

'Nah.'

'Well come on in then.' Billy jumped down and flew past him. When he turned into the hall he couldn't see him among the mass. A group of dads passed the other way, 'Not startin' yet are youse, Ken? Just going fur a wee ciggie.'

'No, you're all right.'

The local councillor, Mary Macdonald, arrived first. She knew the area, knew the flats and their difficulties. She shook Ken's hand and talked about the agenda, anxious that the evening should be about the boys and not develop into a surgery on the ills of the accommodation. Ken said he would keep control. Keith Munroe from Edinburgh, the awards scheme rep, arrived in a taxi. The people gathered in the hall were sorting themselves into seats and there was a sense of expectation. Keith, Mary, Ken and his assistant Hugh, who arrived just in time, took their seats behind the table.

'Git on wi' it, Ken. There's a game later,' someone shouted from the hall.

Ken began the introductions, then gave a short report on the club's activities over the last year: the Reading Project was

Lord of the Flies; the IT group had built a club website; the five-a-side league had played six games, won two and drawn one.

'Now, the reason that we're here…'

'Aye, Celtic kick off in twenty minutes,' called a voice from the hall.

'As many of you here know, we spent a long weekend on the Outer Hebrides at Easter. Twelve boys experienced camping, making their own food, and being self-reliant. All of them learned rock climbing and how to paddle a kayak, and some of them had never seen the open sea before. All the boys on this trip gained enough credits for a bronze award — a splendid achievement.'

They'd straggled in. They wouldn't listen when Mary Macdonald wittered on about the amenities that were being provided, or when the man from the awards scheme talked about future endeavour, but they would take their bronze or silver medal home and hide it from their thieving siblings, or their gran who might pawn it for her next drink.

Keith spoke next, explaining the awards scheme and how it could give the boys entry into college or even university. He talked of the ethos of the organisation as the audience shuffled and coughed; he explained the grants that could be applied for, whilst his listeners (who adhered to the code of 'not for the likes of us') shuffled their feet and coughed.

Finally, Mary was asked to hand over the medals, as Ken gave a description of each winner and what he had accomplished. At the end two names had not been read out.

Billy had sat through it all, dreaming of scoring goals for Celtic, of winning the European Cup, and becoming Scotland's featherweight champion all in the same year, before buying a huge house in North Cumbernauld, with a view of Campsie Fells, where the nobs live. He'd let his mum have a grannie flat as long as she didn't bother him. Right, his name hadn't been called, everyone else had been up — he was off. He scrambled along the row towards the door.

'Not so fast, Billy Logan.'

Billy paused, hearing his name. 'There are two boys who proved on the trip to be outstanding in their thoughtfulness for others, communication skills, their good nature and their willingness to take on any extra duties. They have achieved enough credits to be awarded Silver. Billy Gordon and Mark Fraser, come up to get your medals please.'

Billy saw Mark making his way up the opposite aisle. He changed direction and stepped forward, aware of eyes on him, embarrassed, as if he had been caught nicking sweets from the local shop and was exposed on the high street walking with a policeman. Calls came along the aisle:

'Well done, laddie.'

'Good on yer, Billy.'

Mark reached the front first. He took his prize and shook hands along the table and returned, beaming, to his dad. As Billy arrived the applause swelled; everyone knew Billy. He went along the line, shaking hands and high-fiving Hugh, before turning with a 'whoop' and charging for the door. He could hear the laughter as he got outside.

The chain on the gates of the recycling yard was loose enough to allow him to squeeze through. He sat on an upturned crate for a bit, amongst the debris and stink, then nosed around the broken furniture and old tellies until he heard the crowd leaving. He gave it another ten minutes, pulled up his hood and slipped out. It was nine-thirty, still broad daylight. The medal weighed in the pocket of his jeans. He jumped on a wall, bowed to the Olympic crowd and gave his acceptance speech. Then, to dodge the waiting paparazzi, he headed for the underpass. He sped through the well-known route of tunnels until he emerged in the shopping mall. Yes, they were all there on the bench, sharing a couple of tins and smoking roll-ups.

'Here's the conquering fookin' hero.'

'Gie us a bevvy then.'

'Ye'd better buy wan with yur silver.'

'Ye cannae spend it, yer div.'

'What fookin' use is it then?'

'Here y'are, Bill.' Mark passed him a tin of beer.

'Yer da takin youse to the fitba' tomorrow, Mark?'

'Ay.'

'Fookin' lucky sook.'

'Am no.'

'Stokes gets ten thousand pound every time he plays.'

'Yer talkin' oot yer fanny flaps.'

'Nah, Ah wasnae. Me da told me.'

'He's a fookin' bampot.'

'Where youse goin', Billy?'

'Hame.'

'The polis willnae be here fur 'alf an 'ur.'

'They're here now.'

As the constables approached, Billy kept going. The lads would lark around and cheek the police. It was a nightly ritual; they'd learn stuff, small stuff, swaps; the police would offer a possible empty on their estate for a snitch on a probable break-in. The empty wouldn't be, and the break-in was imagined. Everyone would be happy and the boys would make their way back home.

Billy wasn't obeying the street code. You didn't walk the underpasses alone at night. Last one before his building, most of the lights bashed out, damp, though it hadn't rained to speak of for two weeks. He walked fast, alert, and his feet on the wet concrete heard other feet at the other end, two sets. His heart was pounding. He glanced back — they were in view now, in shadow, men, hands in pockets heads down. Getting closer, don't run, heart thrashing, don't run.

One behind, arm around his neck, his own arm up his back, one in front.

'Wit ye got?'

'Nothin.'

Menacing, face half hidden. 'Ye sure ye havnae got somethin?' Arm pulled up, sharp pain.

'Ah havnae got nothin,' crying, sobbing.

'Ye great jessie.'

'Chib 'im, Con. Chib 'im.'

'Nah, get 'is kecks off.'

He was on the ground, his head held between two knees. Trainers thrown, one pull and jeans ripped off. Something chinked, rolled.

'Whit's tha?'

A lunge, one knee released. Half up, he stumbled, running.

'Ye let the little shite gang awa'. Ah'll gie youse one instead.'

Billy now running, bare feet on gravel, bare legs and arse; a couple coming, stepped aside, stared. Along the walkway, past the hall, the bins, at the next block, up the stairs, familiar stink along the passage. Thump, with his fists.

'Whit's tha? Wha the foo…?'

'It's me, open the fookin' door.' He fell in.

'Jeesus fookin' Christ. Whit's happened to youse? Where's yur troosers?

'Ah just won the fookin' marathon, leave me alone.'

Bedroom door slammed. Billy's mam picked up her glass, left on the side when she opened the door, and emptied it. At the bedroom door, leaning her head against it, she could hear the muffled sobs.

'Did youse get yur award?'

'Nah, naw fook aff and leave me alone.'

'When they prick us, do we not bleed?' Shylock's words were on a loop, like an earworm, impossible to get rid of. Max sat in the chapel. This was respite (nobody came except on Sundays) but it was within bounds in free time. He watched the light play on the pillar in front of the pew. The image was of a reflection of the giant sycamore. The centre of the image was still, and a perfect outline, but the edge of the image was in constant motion. Another window glared onto the pulpit, dominated by the huge bible; the sunbeam's trajectory danced with dust particles. In half an hour the tree vanished and gave place to the precise shape of the window, which gave access to Max, through the plaster and wood of the pillar, to a refuge, a place of no thought.

Earlier he had argued for mercy, the words had been powerful, feminine and commanding, and then suddenly and unexpectedly an erotic fantasy overwhelmed him. He was in the barn in Argentina, but not cowering in a corner, he had taken the place of Joel's conquest. The excitement was intense. At first Portia's words — so well drilled — continued without his assistance:

'His sceptre shows the force of temporal power.'

He smelt the hay beneath him and received Joel with aching desire. He was sweating, and breathing hard. He forgot his words; in the silence the actors in the court-room scene stared at him. Derek was shouting his next line, clearly not for the first time:

'Wherein doth sit the dread and fear of kings… Are you all right, Max?'

The shame of his lust, shame of forgetting his words, of letting Derek down, engulfed him. He bolted from the rehearsal room to where he now sat, calm and safe.

As the performance day drew nearer, Derek suggested the actors should book space in their spare time to work together on their lines.

Max and Ben, who was playing Nerissa, worked at their scenes in every spare moment. Ben was six inches shorter than Max, with black curly hair and a slightly chubby build. Due to his dislike of sport, he too was outside the prominent clique. The two of them had not previously been friends. For two weeks, the boys tentatively engaged with each other, they sat at lunch together and shared prep sessions. In the grounds Max showed secrets: a shrew's nest under rubbish left by the builders; a place where adders basked till they were warm enough to seek their dinner. Ben played the guitar, not well, but Max listened and was encouraging. On rehearsal days, they sat together and afterwards criticised the efforts of the other boys. Their friendship was noticed.

On Sunday afternoon Max waited cross-legged in the middle of the hall for Ben to join him. It was raining outside, heavy summer rain with thunder rumbling in the distance. Ben arrived in a plastic yellow tent and dripped onto the floor.

'Sorry I'm late.'

'That's OK.'

Ben stepped free of his waterfall, which slowly crumpled and stayed like a rocky island in a small pond. He joined Max in the middle of the room.

'Want some gum?'

'I don't think Portia would chew gum.'

'Really? Nerissa does.' He rustled a pack out of his pocket.

'Shall we just do words first?' Max said.

'Sure. You start.'

'By my troth, Nerissa, my little body is aweary of this great world.'

'That's silly'

'What's silly?'

'Well for starters you are not little, and why do you say "aweary"?'

'Portia thinks she is little, maybe she means slim, which I am, and we have to say what Shakespeare wrote even if it seems silly.'

They continued, with Ben stumbling haltingly through his lines, and introducing the suitors in the wrong order, whilst Max fluently produced Portia's much longer speeches. After a couple of goes, Max suggested they stood up and went through the moves that had been directed, adding, 'I think we should practise being women.'

'What do you mean?'

'They walk differently to us.'

'But everyone will know it is us playing them. We don't have to do anything fancy.'

Max found his sports bag at the side of the room and pulled something out.

'I brought these, I think we should try them.' He produced two pairs of high-heeled shoes and placed them side by side: a green pair with a pointed toe and a two-inch heel; and a black pair, slightly higher, with a strap across the instep.

'Where did you get those?'

'I sent off for them from a theatrical costumier; yours are called 'character shoes'. Try them on. Ben hesitated, Max knew what he was asking, and knew that it was daring. Ben removed his trainers and tried one on.

'It doesn't fit.'

'Not with your socks on, it won't. It's your size — I checked.'

Both boys thus clad walked up and down the room. Max, who had practised before, was elegant and serious. Ben, self-conscious, giggling, shoved his bottom out, affecting an exaggerated hip swing.

'Not like that; walk normally.'

'I thought I had to walk like a girl.'

'That's not how girls walk.'

'Fat lot you'd know about it.'

They tried the scene, executing the moves. Max wandered dreamily around, speaking his lines with grace and wit, and slowly drew his other character into concord with him.

Derek was losing confidence in the Merchant of Clydeside. What had seemed such a good idea at the beginning of term now seemed strained and somewhat foolish. He shouted at the actors in rehearsal, demanding more of them than they had any interest in giving. He singled out two boys.

'You play Jessica and Lorenzo like two rugby players, you are not listening to each other, you might as well be reciting the telephone directory.' The two offending actors looked glum and embarrassed.

'Can you not hear the music of the lines? "In such a night, in such a night, in such a night…" This is an intimate scene. I know these days the film version would have them in bed doing rumpy-pumpy, but Shakespeare did it with language.'

The cast appreciated Derek's jokes; he warmed to his task. 'You sound like the commentary on a cricket match, "Thisbe to bowl from the Carthage end, Dido with a willow in her hand, bats it towards the Grecian tents"…' Giggles from the floor.

'Now when Max and Ben play a scene they really talk to one another, you should learn from them. All of you should.'

'We did our best, Sir.'

'Dear God, give me strength! That's all for today. When we meet on Thursday it will be for the first run-through. I want everybody 'off book'. That means *no* prompts. Any free time you have, seek each other out and rehearse. You don't have to use the theatre. There's always space somewhere — the dining hall, the gym, a corridor is room enough for some of the scenes. Just talk to each other, and listen to each other. It is only two weeks to the performance, I hope you realise. Your mums and dads and aunts and uncles, your sister's budgie, and your Australian cousins will be out there so you had better put on a good show.'

'Budgie, Sir?'

Derek smirked, picked up his script and left the rehearsal room.

Och Derek, they dinna ken what a budgie is. Ye should hae said the sister's peacock!

Whisky drew him home, and tomorrow he had the morning free. In front of the television he watched how history is as fickle as showbusiness. If the Russian princesses had not had the measles, the whole of twentieth-century European life would have been different. He fell asleep in his chair and dreamed that Chris was still alive.

Max had watched the rest of the cast as they gathered their things and chatted. Ben asked him if he wanted to listen to some music — Max said he wanted to finish some reading.

Jake, who was playing Bassanio, was last to leave. As he gathered his script and bag, Max approached him.

'Would you like to practise Act Three Scene Two on our own?'

'OK, if you like.'

'How about tomorrow, after prep?'

'Yeah good.'

Jake was six foot, the tallest in the year, just an inch more than Max. He had brown hair, slightly too long for school guidelines, his complexion was marked by acne, yet he was undoubtedly handsome. His upper lip, on which he had a hint of facial hair, was thinner than the lower, and he had a habit of sucking it below its partner. His eyes were brown and challenging and occasionally cruel. He had the well-defined muscular body of a team player, a rugby halfback, a leading batsman. All these respected attributes put him at the heart of the form culture. He, together with Dan and a few others, followed a code of unwritten scruples by which they kept themselves separate and acknowledged in the crowd.

He and his circle established which were the teams to be followed, which players were to be admired, which film stars and other 'celebs' were to be venerated and which despised; all of which could be changed at a moment's notice to catch out an unworthy acolyte. As much as uniform would allow, they were stylish. They had developed nonchalance into an art form. They said they were not virgins. Those who did not conform were nobody; those who aspired to be like them were tolerated and used. Max had always been nobody. Yet Jake had agreed to a one-to-one rehearsal with him.

'I'll book the room for six-thirty p.m.,' Max said.

Jake turned away, picked up his bag and left.

It was six-twenty and Max was still alone in the rehearsal room. He had dressed carefully and casually. He was full of trepidation, much like Portia waiting for her suitor. Jake arrived just after six-thirty.

'Sorry, I didn't know whether you would have waited. I got caught up.'

'That's OK, I was going through my speeches.'

Jake dumped his stuff. 'Good shoes, man.'

Max was wearing low-cut cowboy boots: fine tooled leather, elegant and obviously expensive.

'Thanks.'

'Where did you get them?'

'Buenos Aires. I spent the hols there, on a ranch, with Ma and her boyfriend. He's a polo player.'

Max's heart was racing, he knew he'd scored some points.

'Right, what do you want to do?' Jake found the scene in his script.

'Do you think Portia knows which casket holds her picture?' asked Max.

'She must by now because the other suitors chose the wrong ones,' Jake said.

'Maybe you see me going for the wrong casket and so ask me to wait, and think again?'

'Yes, let's do it like that.'

Jake put out three chairs, to represent the caskets, and as the character of Bassanio, he wandered along touching each one. As he hovered over the last one, Max touched his arm:

'I pray you tarry. Pause a day or two…'

Jake turns to face him, and Max is overcome with emotion, just as Portia is; he lets himself flow into the part, more than he has ever done in previous rehearsals. Jake is a good actor and he listens, and speaks Bassanio's lines with truthful emotion. At the end of the first interchange they are both highly charged, both in a place they've never experienced before.

'Gosh,' said Jake, 'that felt different.'

'I guess that's what it must be like to fall in love.'

There was an awkward pause. Max thought he'd blown it. Jake studied the script.

'Shall we go to when he discovers her picture in the lead casket?' Jake said.

The more formal language of the discovery speech diffused the emotion of the initial interchange. At the end of his speech he looked up to compare the painting he had found in the casket to the real Portia, and gazed into Max's light blue eyes. Max smiled and responding to his own desire and following Shakespeare's genius, in the simplest of language, gave himself to this man. Bassanio replied and moved closer to slip a ring on her finger; then leaning nearer, he lifted his head and kissed Max on the lips.

Max was in turmoil. He was speaking but felt that his tongue was thick and too big for his mouth; the words, whatever they were, were ridiculous and inappropriate to the passion in which he swam like a herring unknowingly entering the dolphin's mouth.

'Maybe best not do that in the real thing,' Jake said.

'No, of course not.' But would you do it again now, he wanted to ask.

'Is that enough for today then?'

'Sure.'

'See you around then.' Jake collected his bag, slung it across his shoulder and left.

Derek parked his car some way down the road from Monica's house. It was a row of Victorian semis on the edge of town, walking distance from the town square, but most people drove. It was the sort of day one would order for a party — sunshine, blue sky, white clouds, not too hot. He could hear music and voices. The front door was open and the noise was coming from the garden. He made his way through the large untidy kitchen. Monica caught sight of him and the chorus of friends parted as she, like an operatic soprano, opened her arms to gather in her man.

'Derek, darling, so glad you made it. I was beginning to think you wouldn't. You naughty boy for being so late.'

Derek felt embarrassed and told a fib about a phone call from Australia he'd had to wait for.

'How intriguing? Now we must get you a drink. Jim's in the garden, serving Pimm's.'

Jim, her much put-upon husband, took his solace in beer. He was standing with a small group of drinking buddies as Monica approached, leading an embarrassed Derek by the hand like a small boy.

'Quiz nights might bring in the punters but they don't necessarily sell the beer. Hello dear, anything I can do?'

'Jim, another guest, Derek's arrived, chop, chop, he must be dying of thirst.' Jim moved behind the table.

'Greetings, Derek, what can I get you?'

'Do you have a lemonade? I've got the car?'

'Have a Pimm's — they are practically non-alcoholic. The girls like them.'

Clearly, he wasn't a real man. Real men drink beer. Derek accepted and moved off, viewing the guests from a side path in the overgrown garden. He knew one or two by sight; they were Chris's old friends — not his type, though he had tolerated occasional pub evenings. The talk was always the same: education, house prices, fear of the new road affecting them. There was nothing intrinsically wrong with the conversation except the boredom that it triggered, which he tended to alleviate with whisky, which inevitably led to a row on the way home.

He caught sight of a woman whose name he knew — Amanda. He remembered her from one of the pub evenings, he found her rather attractive. His opening gambit had been to ask her what she was reading at the time; he remembered her getting flustered and talking about there being too much to do, being too tired in the evenings and how she must get back to books, and what could he recommend?

Then he was stuck as to what titles might interest her. Just now, she caught his eye and waved. He waved back and moved on down the garden to where there had been an attempt at a vegetable patch, but it was now covered in weeds. A fit of enthusiasm in the spring had dwindled as the months progressed: lettuces as tall as pillar boxes; small patches of bare ground where a few carrots had been dug. Blackcurrants ravaged by birds. It felt so typical of Monica; boundary-less, chaotic abundance. 'Food for all' was her motto. Round the end of the raspberry canes and there was Monica's son Matthew, an overweight twelve-year-old who attended the local school. Monica and Jim did not believe in 'private' even though Monica helped at St Edmund's.

'Hello there.'

'Hi.'

He was obviously embarrassed so Derek walked on, smelling cigarette smoke from behind a screen of runner beans. He turned back towards the party and hovered near the group Amanda was in.

'Hello Derek, haven't seen you in ages.'

She introduced him to the rest, though he felt sure he'd met most of them before.

'What have you been doing with yourself?'

'Not a lot really.'

'I hope you haven't been staying in and getting morbid.'

'No, of course not.'

'Well you must join our quiz night. Thursdays at the Crown and Sceptre.'

'Ah, "the attribute to awe and majesty".'

'What's that?' said one of the group.

'Derek's frightfully clever, we need him on our team.'

'But I don't know anything about soaps and celebrities'

'That's all right, we've got that covered.'

The conversation moved off in another direction and Derek stood listening. Alienated, he knew how Max must have felt at the beginning of term. Max was happier these days, more integrated now he was in the play. He even seemed to have found a friend in Ben — another outsider but that was all to the good. No boats would be rocked.

Derek noticed a few of the guests were beginning to say their goodbyes; most had been there for a couple of hours before he arrived. He scanned the guests as the crowd on the lawn began to thin. He must be here somewhere. Then he saw him — it had to be him — laughing with a group of women, a tallish man about his own age, wearing immaculate white jeans, a new sports shirt still with the creases in it, and a pair of sunglasses balanced on his head. What a dick, he thought. How could she? A teenager passed by and offered Derek a sausage while her friend replenished his drink. A hand on his shoulder:

'Monica?'

'I'm going to call Tony over — it's crazy you two haven't met.'

She approached the laughing group, and whispered in Tony's ear. Derek watched as he extricated himself from the acolytes to obey Monica.

'Hello, are you Derek Baker?'

'Yes, I am.'

'Now you two will have so much to talk about. Forgive me, I must say goodbye to Bob and Clara.'

'I'm Tony Belcher, I run the sports shop on the high street.'

'I know.'

'I knew Chris very well, I was her tennis coach.'

'I know.'

'Funny we never met, I wanted to talk to you at the funeral, I so admired her, she was a marvellous woman, and so brave, you must miss her dreadfully. I know I do. I mean, not in the same way as you, but she was such a lively presence at the club. You don't play tennis yourself?'

'No. That will be why we've never met.'

'Tony.' A female voice called across the grass.

'Coming, darling.'

'Would that be Mrs Belcher?'

'No, not Mrs! Maybe one day. Managed to avoid it so far. Come and meet her.'

'Not just now.'

Tony lifted one tailored leg onto a low wall and thrust one hand deep in his trouser pocket. The change of position shifted his sunglasses and they fell in the weeds. Derek watched as he retrieved them. Flustered, he rose to face Derek's cold stare.

'Well, I'm glad I've spoken to you, hope to see you around.'

'Did you know that Chris kept a journal?'

'No. I mean why should I…'

'Yes, she recorded everything, all the matches, even the scores sometimes, forty-love, deuce, that sort of thing. Some things she left for me to read afterwards.'

'After…?'

'Yes, after she died.'

'Oh, you mean? Gosh, look I don't think… I mean, it was nothing.'

'Adultery never is…anything.'

'A fling.'

'Yes. That's what she called it. You know what I most despise about you? It's that you thought it was within the bounds of decency to approach me today. Was it to gloat? To discover what a difference you'd made? Well, it made no difference. You made no difference. Turds like you will always be around to take advantage of a vulnerable moment in a relationship. You seek it out, fertilise it with the shit of your imagined charisma, to force it. But as regards being important, or having any significance, or meaning anything beyond a quick shag, forget it.'

And Derek turned, made his way up the side passage and out of the front garden without bidding anyone goodbye. He heard Monica calling:

'Derek? Are you going?' He didn't turn. 'So glad you met Tony… Bye.'

He started the car and found he was heading out towards the Beacon. Radio Three was playing jazz He turned it up loud and beat his hands on the steering wheel. Maybe he hadn't said all he'd imagined himself saying, over and over, on many post-whisky evenings, but he'd said enough. He'd called him a turd; the stupid schoolboy expression was perfectly apt for the peacocked shit. Derek felt a man again, mission accomplished. He got out of the car at the top and sat for a while watching the dog walkers, the picnickers, the lovers on the grass. All right he was lonely but the Internet could fix that when he was ready. Right now he needed a plan that would get him away from this town and this deadening job.

He parked the car back at school at about five o'clock. He'd eaten nothing at the party and his fridge was empty. Maybe he'd go out again later to the Indian. As he turned the corner of the building someone stepped from the bushes. It was Max.

'What are you doing here? You know this is off limits.'

'I had to see you.'

'Well?' Max hesitated, Derek waited.

'I can't be in the play. I'm backing out.'

'What?! Why?'

Max was rigid and Derek feared him retreating into one of his seemingly catatonic states. 'You'd better come inside.'

They sat at the table in Derek's small kitchen, Max still bolt upright and hardly breathing. Derek made two mugs of tea, put loads of sugar in Max's, and waited. Twenty minutes passed on the microwave clock before Max, in hardly more than a whisper, said 'Sorry'.

'You have to tell me what has happened, Max.'

He was still unforthcoming. Derek made fresh tea and continued, 'I suppose it can happen that a cast member gets an illness that prevents him performing, or he could have an accident or a bereavement, and in any of those cases the school and the rest of the cast would be sympathetic, and another boy would be found to read in his lines and it would go ahead in a much diminished way. Have any of those things happened to you, Max?'

'No.'

'Then I don't understand.'

'I have heard from my mother, she is planning to come to the play.'

'Well, that's wonderful. Surely you don't want to let her down?'

'She is bringing her boyfriend, Tobias, with her.'

'Max I don't understand, you will have to explain some more.'

Max's face was working like a neglected pan of stew, burning at the bottom and exploding at the top.

'He said I was a "patsy" for playing a girl.'

'But in a boys' school someone always has to play the female roles.'

'He says you always choose the "patsies".'

'What does he mean by "patsy"?' Max did not answer. 'Do you think he means homosexual?'

'I suppose so.'

'And will he think that Ben is a "patsy" for playing Nerissa? And Simon for playing Jessica?'

'Yes… No.'

'Just you, eh?'

'Yes.'

It had occurred to Derek that Max might be gay, in the way that one did sometimes wonder about a boy; idle speculation, of no consequence. Boys were put three to a room to try and counter close relationships, though there must be boys who experimented. Why not? It would happen in a co-educational school across both genders. Derek felt he was aware and free of the prejudices still held by some of the school staff.

'You were going to write about your holiday in Argentina. Did you ever do that?'

'No.'

'Well I was going to write about the Hebrides and I never did that. You know we have a school counsellor, maybe you could talk about this with her.'

'Do you think I'm gay?'

'I have no idea? How would I know? Do you know?'

'Yes, I think I am — no — I am.' Max bent his head and put his hand across his face.

'Max, look at me. It is perfectly all right, completely normal, natural.' Derek felt weak, he was hungry; the emotions of the afternoon's encounter with Belcher, followed by this, were wasting him. Yet he couldn't dismiss the boy.

'Where are you supposed to be, Max?'

'In the lower common room or in my study room. I won't be missed till bedtime.' It was six-thirty — they had three hours.

'Shall we go for a meal?'

This was rash on Derek's part and seriously compromised school rules.

'I don't mind.'

The familiar phrase disarmed him, Max had tears in his eyes. Derek, careless of rules again, hugged him.

'You'll have to keep your head down in the car.'

Derek didn't drive into town. There was an Indian restaurant in a village in the other direction and it would be very unlucky if they bumped into someone from school there. The waiters knew him by sight; they called him 'Sir' and Max 'Young Sir'. By now Max was relaxed and in his own way enjoying himself. Indian food was new to him, as was dining with a master.

'Do you think there are other boys in school like me?'

'In respect of their sexuality you mean?'

Max looked at his plate.

'Do you mean other boys who are gay?' Max nodded. 'Undoubtedly; but you are all young and in some cases their sexual identity will not have become an issue.'

'I think Jake is.'

'What makes you think that?'

'We were rehearsing by ourselves and he kissed me.' Max blushed deeply. Derek knew Jake, and his ilk; they were invincible, arrogant, prepared to use any situation for their own warped sense of entertainment.

'Anything else?'

'No. But if he's … gay… then maybe it's all right for me to be.'

'I don't think that follows at all. It's all right for you to be gay, whether or not certain others are or may be. It is a natural thing. It is a manly thing. But dear Max you are too young as yet to experiment, and in the close-knit atmosphere of school it could lead to all sorts of hurt. When you are older and at university, that will be the time to find others who share your inclinations. There you will have a wonderful time and find many lovers. Maybe boys, maybe girls. Right now, in school, you must keep your own counsel. Promise me.'

'If you like.'

'No, promise me.'

'I promise.'

'And are you going to be in the play?'

'If you like.'

'Max?'

'Yes, I am.'

'Meanwhile, don't rehearse on your own with Jake again. Find an excuse if he asks.'

'OK.'

As the performance drew nearer, Derek kept as close an eye as possible on his cast whilst continuing normal school duties. As Dr Hudson was fond of pointing out, curriculum did not cease, and exam boards made no exceptions for boys involved in dramatics.

The dress rehearsal was on Wednesday evening, Thursday was a day off, Friday they would have a school audience and Saturday, parents and friends.

The art department had done wonders transforming an ex-ballroom turned assembly hall into Clydeside docks, with an enormous cargo ship on one of three painted cloths, the second representing a courtroom and the third a classical garden (supposedly Portia's country estate in Fife). Now it was the boys' turn to see their costumes, all neatly hung in rows in the gym with character names attached.

'I'm not wearing a fucking kilt,' Daniel exploded.

'I beg your pardon, young man?' Monica was helping out backstage.

'Sorry but I'm not wearing a skirt.'

'It's not a skirt, it's a kilt, and if it's good enough for royalty then it's good enough for you.'

'Looks like I've got one too,' Jake said.

Max found Portia's name on the rail. He had two costumes; the first was a pair of wide silk trousers in gold with a dark brown sash and a cream shirt. This was for the early scenes, when he meets Bassanio. The second was a dark blue business suit, with wide lapels, for when he was acting the lawyer. He would return to his first costume for the final act of the play.

'Look Max has got trousers and he's playing a woman.'

'God, he must be disappointed,' came from an anonymous voice.

'Ha' ye got a bra there, hen?'

Max froze for a second, caught Ben's grinning face and grinned back.

'I think Bassanio must fancy flat-chested women.'

'Is that so, Jaky?' said Ben.

'I thought youse was a boob man,' contributed Dan in his best camp Glaswegian. And so the banter continued as the boys struggled into their costumes and fought for the mirror. Ben looked ridiculous in a big flowered shirt-waister dress, Jake looked magnificent in his kilt and sporran. Dan as Launcelot Gobbo, in threadbare kilt, darned fisherman's jumper, bare legs and workman's boots, had changed his mind and thought his get-up the best of everyone's.

The dress rehearsal and technical rehearsal happened at the same time, so it was a very stop-start affair, with lights having to be refocused, and sound cues altered or refined. The boys got alternately over-excited and fractious and at eleven p.m. Dr Hudson arrived to find out why all was not quiet and why the boys were not in their dorms. Naturally he blamed Derek, who promised they would be in bed in half an hour. At eleven-forty-five, Monica was picking costumes off the gym floor whilst the cast, encouraged by helpful staff members, made a dash for their various houses.

On Saturday night in the gym, getting ready for their second performance, the noisy excitement of the boys ceased suddenly as the presence of their headmaster seeped through the room. Daniel, in his underpants and Doc Martins, was attempting a Scottish dance with Ben, who saw and froze. Daniel spun round. 'Good afternoon, Sir.' Hudson ignored him.

'Well, boys! Very well done last night. A thoroughly enjoyable performance! Mrs Hudson is coming tonight and she was an actress years ago so she will be a critical audience, but if you pull it off like last night she will be impressed. As will all your parents. So carry on, and "break a leg".'

Muffled mumbles of 'thank you sir' issued from amongst the clothes rails.

Hudson bumped into Derek who was on his way to the gym on a similar errand.

'Ah Derek!' Hudson boomed. 'Sorry I didn't catch you last night. Very well done. Come down to the office when you've seen the boys.'

In a small way, in a small environment, Derek had triumphed. Colleagues had been seeking him out to praise him, and now Hudson, whose default position was mildly disapproving, was full of praise. There was little in the past to relate this feeling to, except perhaps his early days with Christabel. Not since then had he felt such a sense of conquest.

He saw the boys, gave them a few notes and geed them up, unnecessarily. Derek had no interest in cars, but on the way to Hudson's room he saw the procession of latest-model top of the range cars arriving in the school quad, disgorging their groomed and ostentatious occupants towards the reception marquee.

'Sit down, have a drink. Whisky? Sherry?'

Derek said he'd have a sherry. Hudson's room was on the first floor. Originally a drawing room, it was book-free, dominated by his desk, with a window onto the school gardens and beyond to the tennis courts.

'Cheers Derek, and as I said, very well done. Some of those boys gave superb performances. Young Jake, eh? Glad we didn't join with the girl's school, with a chap like that at large. And you have done wonders with young Max; he hardly spoke a word when he first came. And when he did, you couldn't hear it. Really good work. We should have a chat, maybe give drama a bit more curriculum space, eh?'

Derek saw a Rolls park at the side of the tennis courts and a woman, unquestionably Max's mother, get out. Mother and son were so alike, at this distance and with Max as a girl, they would be taken for twins. She was wearing a pair of jeans, with a shirt and linen jacket.

'What do you reckon? Might encourage more of them to do Drama GCSE?'

'Yes, I'd be very happy to take that on.'

What was he saying? Until his recent elation, he'd been planning to leave as soon as notice could be served.

'Well, better get down to the reception, rattle the bucket for the new tennis school, eh? Finish your drink and join me downstairs, I'll introduce you as our drama director.'

He downed his sherry in one go and hurried out.

An awning had been erected outside the hall and senior boys were serving champagne. There were around sixty parents and friends standing in groups. Derek could see Mrs Henderson and her guest, a tall muscled, dark man in casual clothes, possibly her junior. Hudson was talking to them as he waved Derek over.

'Come and meet Max's parents.'

Derek did as he was told.

'This is Derek Baker who directed the play; we've just been saying what a wonderful little performer Max is. He has really developed in confidence this term, and that shows in all his results. Not much of a sportsman, but never mind, they just need to excel in something.'

Mel held out an elegant, bejewelled hand. Tobias caught no one's eye but merely acknowledged Hudson with a slight inclination of his head and scanned the room over Derek's left shoulder.

A small balding fat man, with a wife to match, had Derek in range. 'I think you must be Mr Baker?'

Derek turned to face them; and the beautiful couple moved away with Hudson in tow, having not spoken a word to Derek.

'Indeed.'

'We are Daniel's mum and dad, or should I say Gobbo's parents? He really has had great fun with this part. Even got us reading the play!'

'Well, he is a splendid actor, and comedian.'

'Oh yes, we know that all right,' said the maternal half, lifting her thinly tweezered eyebrows to just under her delicately dyed fringe. 'Quite a comedian.'

A fat child of around eight or nine was hovering. Mr Gobbo introduced him.

'This is Ruben, he'll be joining you soon, I think you'll find him another contender for the school play.'

Ruben looked Derek straight in the eye.

'Yeah, I think acting is great, 'specially in pantomime. We're putting on *Jack and the Beanstalk* at Grenville and I'm playing Jack.'

'Well done.'

'I run a small acting group in our village,' said Mrs Gobbo. 'Very amateur, but we have lots of fun. I persuaded David to play the wizard,' she said, referring to Mr Gobbo. 'Well, see you after the show. Break a leg and all that.'

They moved away, joining the now considerable crowd progressing into the hall.

There was an expectant buzz of conversation in the auditorium. Derek stood at the back, he twitched, his eyes involuntarily blinked with great speed. This always happened when he was stressed.

The small school orchestra (two violins, a viola, some woodwind and a piano) was playing a medley of Scottish tunes. Derek had not been consulted. 'The Skye Boat Song' and 'The Gay Gordons' — he winced at the inappropriateness of the selection as well as at every wrong note. It lasted ten minutes, after which the young players took a bow, over enthusiastic and thoroughly undeserved applause. Younger boys then removed the music stands and pushed the piano to the side. The audience was quietly expectant as the curtain rose on the painted backcloth of the Clyde, with opening characters, Salerio and Salanio, dressed as dockworkers trying to jolly up Antonio, their boss.

Not a brilliant opening scene and Derek had cut it to a minimum. As the other characters joined, especially Jake as Bassanio, Derek and the audience relaxed. The next scene was Portia and Nerissa (Max and Ben). The audience was revelling in Ben's pantomime performance; there had been little choice but to let Ben turn Nerissa into a comedy role, especially in his ridiculous costume. Shylock made his appearance as a mafia godfather in competition with Antonio. All was going well. Next the scene between Bassanio and Portia. Derek knew would impress, it was superb acting by any standards. The audience seemed hardly to breathe whilst Jake chose the casket and revealed Portia's picture.

Bassanio was speaking:

'…But when this ring

Parts from this finger, then parts life from hence:

O, then be bold to say Bassanio's dead!'

This was Ben's cue to announce the arrival of Bassanio's friend Gratiano. There was a titter of delighted expectation from the audience as he appeared, followed by audible gasps and a female scream. Jake had stepped forward, embraced Max and was kissing him passionately on the lips. Voices repeating and getting louder.

'DISGUSTING!'

Parents on their feet, pushing for the door, dragging the actors' younger siblings with them.

Derek was first out and running along the corridor towards the backstage entrance. The kiss was over and the two boys were apart and staring at each other. He bellowed for the curtain to come down; he saw Jake, his face in a seeming sneer, turn his back on Max and head for the wings. Max was alone, in shock, traumatised by what had happened. He turned to look at Derek, tears spilling onto his silk top.

'You'd better go to the gym, Max. It's not your fault.' He could hear Paul's voice backstage.

'All to the gym immediately and get changed. You are to stay there until further notice.' Choruses of 'Why, Sir?' 'What's happened, Sir?'

'Do as you are told immediately.' Paul saw Derek onstage.

'Bloody hell — did you know that was coming?'

'Of course I fucking didn't.'

'Now, now, keep your hair on.'

'What's happening out there?'

'Hudson's holding the fort, calming quite a lot of hysteria, there are parents wanting to call the police.'

'The police?'

'Well they are under-age, Derek.'

'Yes, but it wasn't bloody coitus!'

'I wouldn't say that out there. In fact Hudson said if I saw you to tell you to keep a low profile. I should shuffle off if I was you. Let him handle it.'

Paul slipped through the curtains into the auditorium. Derek was furious. Paul, Head of Art, a closet queen if ever there was one, was in his element.

The parental atmosphere was tense and silent in the reception. In contrast the boys were buzzing with the glee of wrongdoing. Only Ben had witnessed the offence, but his powers of description had been amply rewarded by the coterie surrounding him, and additional tales of transvestism swelled his account. Melly welcomed Max with kisses. Tobias ignored him.

In the car, Spanish music inappropriately serenaded the silent anger of Tobias and the undeserved shame of Max. His simultaneous attraction to and loathing of Tobias was a toxic mix too powerful for the boy to understand. At the country hotel the dining room was still open and almost empty. Tobias led the way to a table, and dealt with menus and wine. Max fixed his eyes on the pattern of the window curtain — a grey background with classical scenes printed in a rococo frame. He entered the frame and sat at the foot of a goddess playing a lyre, he fondled her dog.

'Darling. Max, Max!'

Melly shook his arm, he was unaware of her calling. Roused, something released in his diaphragm and a rush of air seemed to set him spinning and floating above the table whilst they talked below him.

'Leave it, Tobias. We can talk tomorrow.'

'We have to get to the bottom of this.'

'Yes, tomorrow.'

'I'm not having him going back to that school — he can come to Argentina with us.'

'You know his father won't allow that.'

'Even when he hears what happened tonight?'

'Leave it, Toby.'

The conversation ceased and after a while Max floated down onto his chair. Melly chatted about developments on the ranch with a forced normality. The other two (one feeling that by association his manhood had been challenged; and the other, returning to the woman and her small dog, reliving with thumping heart every nuance of the kiss, the heat, the smell, the pressure, the push) made no response.

Later on, Melly came into his room to say goodnight. She sat on the bed and held his hand and told him that they were going for an interview with Mr Hudson tomorrow and that it would be easier if they had a little talk now.

'I'm sorry you didn't see all the play, Mummy. It was really awfully good, especially the courtroom scene. You know "the quality of mercy is not strained".'

'Yes, I'm sorry too.'

'You missed Dan being so funny. He will be furious that his mum and dad didn't see it. Do you think they'll let us do it again?'

'I shouldn't think so, darling.'

'I wish Jake hadn't done that stupid thing.'

'Did you know he was going to do it?'

'No.'

'Had he done it before?'

'He did it once, in rehearsal.'

'So Mr Baker knew about it?'

'He didn't think it was a good idea to put it in the performance, so I was really surprised.'

'You like Mr Baker, don't you? You stayed with him at half-term. Did you like his wife?'

'She's dead. I think he's been really lonely. We used to go on long walks, and have fish and chips and Indian meals and talk about poetry and stuff.'

'Is this when you were staying with him?'

'Yes, and after sometimes.'

He looked up at his mother, and followed her gaze to a book on his bedside table for reading later, *This Book Is Gay.*

She reached for it. 'Do you think you are gay, Max?'

'I think I might be.'

'Where did you get this book?'

'Mr Baker gave it to me — he thought it might be useful.'

'So you talked about this subject with him? Why was that? Had you asked him?'

Max remembered the rehearsal with Jake and his bewilderment.

'I think it was all to do with the play.'

'I see.'

'No, you don't. You think the same as him. Mr Baker said being gay was a normal manly thing.' Melly flicked through the book and noticed a handwritten inscription on the flyleaf. 'Dear Max, I hope this is helpful, with best wishes, Derek Baker.'

She leant over and kissed him.

'I think you are too young to know about these things yet. See you in the morning. You needn't come and see Hudson with us, you can lark about in the grounds here. Night night, darling.'

Sunday, grey sky, warm with a slight drizzle. The rain stopped at about two p.m., when Derek went out for a walk. He thought incessantly about what had happened. Had the boys colluded? He felt that was not the case and that Jake, without doubt, had done it for sheer devilment. Well, he'd definitely be in favour of expulsion.

He was walking the same route he had taken with Max five months before. Then the boy had been wary, introverted, withdrawn. How vulnerable these boys were. He saw his own boyhood confusions being played out and wondered whether the years had released him from his demons or just buried them deeper. He walked, considering a crime, himself the accused, conducting the interrogation. He admitted that Max, yes, had become perhaps overly attached to him, and yes, he scrutinised himself, it was reciprocated. He loved the boy. He had taken the place of Chris who during her illness had been vulnerable and responsive to his love. Max had exposed his own adolescence, confused and defenceless. Through Max he had begun to heal himself. The timing was perfect, there was emptiness after Christabel, a crack for love to slide in, and he had not foreseen it.

The earlier rainfall had made the rocks slippery, even above the tide line. Derek remembered Max collecting his trophies and the orange Sainsbury's bag, and wept.

He began his walk back, clambering from the rocks to the shingle beach. Damn, a group was walking towards him, two adults and two boys larking around with a dog. He was caught. This was bound to be a family from the school, parents who had seen the debacle. He braced himself for at least a 'good afternoon' and hoped that would be all. He saw Dan first, who ran back to his parents. They looked his way and called their younger son to them. The family passed wordlessly. Derek was puzzled. Naively it had not occurred to him that he should shoulder any blame for the malicious act of a young hooligan.

The rest of the beach was deserted, as was the track back to school. His success, a flame in the wind, was now extinguished in embarrassment and humiliation. Fucking Daniel Grosch and his fucking self-satisfied parents. Back in the flat it was time for oblivion from the bottle and a couple of DVDs.

Monday morning, hung over, he stared at his blotched face as he shaved. It was time he stopped drinking, but how many times had he thought that before? Bereavement was a reasonable excuse, but had it got out of hand?

His first class was English language with Form One B. He skipped assembly and reached the classroom just before the bell for the start of the morning's session. Miss Dancer was at the front; she was a teaching assistant who moved around, helping with various classes. Derek was pleased to see her. A bit of support this morning was just what he needed.

'Good morning, Derek. Mr Hudson said would you go and see him in his office? He said for me to hold the fort here.'

She smiled, a concealing smile. 'Is there anything you want me to set them?'

Derek told her where they'd reached in the grammar textbook and left the room as the boys streamed in. At least they seemed pretty normal.

Reaching Hudson's office, he opened the door.

'Sit down, Baker. Sit down.'

Surname, Derek thought. What the fuck's this about?

'Bit of a fiasco on Saturday night, eh?'

'Indeed, though some of the hysteria was a bit of an over-reaction, I thought.'

'You did, did you?'

Derek sensed he should be warier but clung on…

'Well, Paul said they were demanding that the police be called.'

'It was a difficult situation to contain and one I fear will have repercussions. I wonder if you could tell me how the incident came about?'

'You mean the kiss?'

'Of course I mean the bloody kiss.'

Christ, he was being blamed. 'Well … I suppose Jake just decided to do it … sheer bloody-mindedness.'

'There had been no mention of a kiss before.'

'No.'

…not granite but sandstone — he was slipping.

'According to Mrs Henderson and Max's step-father, you directed the kiss…'

'What?'

'You have taken Max out of school, for meals, just the two of you. Whilst staying alone, alone, with you in your flat, over half-term, which was completely out of order, you persuaded him to play the part of Portia. You have discussed and explained homosexuality to the boy, and the lovers he could expect to have, and even lent him a book on the subject!'

Derek was silent in his fury of confusion. He bit his lip to feel the pain, something he had not done since he was a teenager. However much the facts had been twisted, and by whom, it was clear that Max had for some reason let him down.

'You asked me to have Max for half-term, and I don't believe you were unaware of my marital (or lack of marital) status.'

'I thought your sister was still staying with you.'

'Bollocks.'

How could he explain? How could he now admit that the boy had become close, that he Derek had befriended him, had brought him out into school society? How could anything he said now sound innocent?

'Do you mean you really believe that I told the boys to kiss?'

'I believe things might have gone on in rehearsal that could have led to it.'

Derek wondered just how bloody sly Jake had managed to be when Hudson interviewed him.

'Jake's parents were not there on Saturday, but I shall be writing to them. The Hendersons are demanding something be done about it, and Daniel's parents are threatening to go to the press unless…'

'Unless what?'

Neither man spoke. Derek now determined that Hudson should say it.

'Well, a resignation is called for…'

'I see.'

'With immediate effect.'

'And will that be with or without a reference?'

'I think that might be quite difficult in these circumstances.'

'Then fucking sack me and we'll see what the press think of that. I think it would make something of a story, if only for the local press, or the odd tabloid, I can see the headline. I have absolutely nothing to hide, so I'll leave it in your capable hands.'

'I don't think you need to take that attitude.'

'You don't? You don't care to enquire about my side of things? You don't know that according to the Kinsey report, back in the 1950s, ten per cent of the population are homosexual, so it is likely that ten per cent of the boys under your care are homosexual, as no doubt were ten per cent of the men of you served with in the Royal Marines — before you took to education — but you prefer to believe that it is just the odd pervert who can be reclaimed for the good of England, the Church and all who sail in her. Yes, you can have my resignation. As it happens, I was going to leave anyway at the end of the year; a term earlier is fine by me. So you can have it, but only when I am happy with your reference.'

There were three weeks to go until the end of term. Miss Dancer took over One B. The Hendersons and the Groszs, ringleaders of the 'heads must roll campaign', had stipulated no teaching, so the rest of Derek's time was taken with invigilating the end of term exams, and packing — though just what he was packing for remained undecided. His sister would store the furniture in her garage whilst he sorted himself out. He was relieved she didn't offer him a bed.

Shortly before term ended there was a get-together in the senior staff common room; beer and sandwiches, desultory speeches, how much he'd be missed and other platitudes. On the last day most boys were collected, dragging their kit in overflowing badly packed bags to the waiting cars. A few boys had to wait another day for the convenience of their drivers. Max was one of these. When Derek took a last walk to the memorial garden, which he thought likely he would never see again, he saw the boy on the bench.

A stipulation of the reference had been no contact with Max Henderson, but Derek cared little. He waited by the rose garden for Max to speak. It was a perfect English summer's day, a few dainty clouds on a perfectly blue cloth, the sun beaming and the roses smelling like roses. Derek deadheaded a few as he waited. He knew Max would speak, he knew that was why Max was there, and was not ignorant of it feeling like a tryst.

'Hello Max.'

'Hello Derek.'

'I haven't seen you for a while.'

'No. How were the exams?'

'All right. Are you leaving?'

'Yes.'

'Why?' It was Derek's turn to be silent. 'Is it my fault?'

Their eyes caught for an instant and then Max looked down again. He looked too thin. Derek noticed the red weals down his thumbs where he had picked away the skin.

'No, it's not your fault.'

'I think I said some things to Mother that I shouldn't have.'

'Don't worry about that. They needed someone to blame, I was handy.'

'I wanted to say thank you.'

'That's very nice of you. What for exactly?'

'I suppose for being my friend. Will we stay friends?'

The innocence whipped his back, and the pain made him angry.

'You are a schoolboy, and I'm an out of work schoolmaster, and soon we will be miles apart and have no knowledge of each other's lives.'

Max sobbed, and Derek still lashed, 'And besides I have been forbidden to see you.'

'Why! Who did that? They can't do that!'

Derek relented. 'I will think about you often. I wish I could take you through many wonderful texts and poems and see you getting A-stars, and reading English at university, because that is what you'll do. And then you will be your own man and people will not push you around. Beware the Jakes of this world.'

Then without caution Derek hugged the boy.

Just beyond the rose garden Max caught up with him and gave him an envelope before running on in the direction of the main school building.

Back in his empty flat Derek opened the envelope. A single sheet in Max's handwriting.

…Who then devised the TORMENT? Love.
Love is the unfamiliar Name
Behind the hands that wove
The intolerable shirt of flame …

Derek knew the quote from T. S. Eliot's *Quartets*. It helped but not in the way that Max had intended it to, as a declaration, but because the complicated fantasies of this adolescent boy were being explored through literature, as many had done before him; and Derek recognised himself.

He picked up his suitcase; it was time to leave this chapter.

PART TWO

Chapter 1. Billy

'Billy, will youse git up noo? It's eleven o'clock an we've got tae go doon yer Gran's. Ah kin dae withoot the auld bugger complainin'. Ye ken whit she's like.'

'Fook aff Ma, will ye?'

'Ah'll come in an drag youse!'

'Ye wouldnae fookin' dare!'

His mother heard some bumping and dragging; he was barricading the door.

'Well if ye want yer dinner, ye'd bettur git yer keks on an' folly me soon.'

Billy heard the door slam and crawled back under his smelly duvet. His ma was a regular at the launderette and sometimes helped out there if one of the girls was off, but she hadn't been allowed in Billy's room for about a year. She'd sometimes give him a set of bedclothes to change it himself but he seldom bothered.

He gave his mother ten minutes and then shifted his dresser from the door and went to the kitchen where he pulled drawers open, rummaged, and shoved things back in. He wasn't entirely sure what he was looking for. He took some candle ends, some brown wrapping paper, a knife and a crayon. He had matches in his room. He left his cache neatly on top of his dresser, dressed quickly and — taking a shopping bag —

left the house. He retraced his steps from last night. There were people about but Billy moved through them as a spectre might, being invisible by nature of his total ordinariness, and feeling invisible, by nature of his faith in the extraordinary. He slid into the tunnel, not exactly sure where he'd find them, but convinced he would. Keeping to the wall, he sidled along. There they were, lying as clothes sometimes do in odd public places, waiting to tell a story that no one asks. He picked up his trousers and put them in his bag.

Back in his room he spread the paper on the top of the dresser and with the crayon in his child-like hand drew two figures. He arranged the trousers so that each leg draped down one side of the drawings. Then he lit the candles and traced wax from the trousers to each figure, then left them burning at the side. With the knife, he stabbed the first picture in its torso:

'Ye'll no' keep ma medal,' then repeated it with the second. 'That's the first pain, it'll git worse till ah git ma medal back,' and he stabbed the knife in between the two figures and left it there.

'Youse'uv been warned.'

He had an idea in his head, like a television 'reconstruction' that was meant to jog memories about who was around when a crime was committed; someone dressed up as the victim and walked the walk at the same hour of the day or night the 'incident' had happened. He didn't need a memory jog, he was the victim, and he wasn't going to walk, bold as brass, through that tunnel again at this deserted time.

Nevertheless he was there from nine-thirty, concealed by a bush at the entrance to the tunnel — one of those totally unkempt shrubs found in neglected parts of any city, or motorway verge, planted by the Council to humanise a dead landscape, leggy roses with black spot on their few remaining leaves and single buds swollen with damp and disease; Berberis and Skimmia that would never bloom, amenity planting to suck up carbon monoxide; such a nameless straggler Billy hid behind, convinced that the two men who had attacked him and stolen his medal would repeat their journey. It was ten-fifteen when he saw them coming towards him — he was in no doubt it was them. He'd timed the tunnel, three minutes to the other end, he was not going to get trapped. When the time was up, he ran soundlessly, lightly, his feet like springs coiled with willpower.

At the far end of the tunnel he could see them entering the mall. The shops were shuttered for the night, all except one, a newsagent which still had lights on. The two men went inside. Must need fags or a can of lager, Billy thought. He hid in shadows keeping watch. They were in a while — too long — he thought he'd missed them somehow. Ten minutes passed. As he slipped out of hiding, the men finally appeared. They looked briefly in his direction, saw him, an invisible youngster in a hoodie, and having no interest in him, carried on. They walked fast in the other direction. He would tail them if it took all night.

He drew level with the newsagent, one of the men looked round as though worried he was being followed, and Billy slipped into the shop to avoid being seen. There was no one behind the counter. He'd only been there a few seconds when he heard a groan from the back and knew in an instant the whole scenario. He found Mr Hussein lying behind the counter, with a little pool of blood forming by his head. The till was open and empty, and the cigarette shelves stripped. It was not the first time Mr Hussein had been beaten for the day's takings. Now he banked in the afternoon, leaving his daughter in charge; but small pickings had not deterred these two. Billy found the shop phone and called the police. He didn't give his name but said he'd wait. Old Hussein continued to groan. Billy sat by his head and talked to him, and told him it would be all right.

'Dinnae fash yersel', the ambulance will be here in five.'

The old man was shaking. Billy touched him and he felt cold. He took off his hoodie and put it over him. It was not much use. He wandered round the shop to find something that might keep him warm. Woolly hats, a new line hung above the counter, and he did his best to pull one over his bloodied head. There was nothing like a blanket. He pulled the largest aluminium foil off the shelves and covered the man like an oven-ready turkey.

'Hang on, Mester. They'll sort youse oot at tha 'ospital.'

Billy held his hand. 'Ah ken the bastarts that did ye. Ah ken whit they look like, an Ah ken wan o' thair names.'

Billy could hear the sirens in the distance, and as the sounds closed in he had visions of himself, on the TV and in the newspaper: 'Young lad's bravery saves old man. Read the full story.' Then he saw the faces of Callum and his pal. He was a dead man. They'd come for him.

The screaming cars were just outside. Their headlights pierced the shop, bounced off the foil, and lit the blood now almost reaching the door. Billy cowered behind one of the displays, as the first two officers entered the shop. In his invisible disguise, he slid out. He waited some time behind the bins, the ambulance arrived and after a while they carried the old man out on a stretcher. Billy slid into an alley that led behind the shop, waited a moment, and then legged it to the tunnel.

He let himself into the flat, quietly, though it would have made little difference if he'd knocked the door in; his mother, snoring in front of the blaring TV, would not have woken. His room was as he had left it. The hex, draped with his trousers and fixed by the kitchen knife was untouched.

Stripping quickly, he burrowed into bed in his underpants. Sinking deeper, lights flashed and metallic tearing made his fingernails quiver. The men shouted as they rolled him in tin-foil. He had to bite into the metallic element to keep an airway, forcing his fingers and nails through layer after layer, always to find more. He tore at it with his teeth and his mouth filled with the taste and texture of aluminium. Waking, he threw back his cover. Soon his sweat turned to a freezing slime and he found his cover again, drawing it to his chin as he sat upright and dared not close his eyes. The window, high up in the wall opposite his bed, threw a city-yellow glare on the chest and its assemblage. As his eyes drooped, so the faces of Callum and his partner appeared, leering from the dresser. At one point they took up the trousers and with the knife slit then in half. Billy felt the knife separate his ribs and screamed in the darkness. By morning he was exhausted.

'Billy, Billy, are ye up yit? It's nearly half eight, ye'll miss the skool bus. Billy? Billy?'

'Ah'm no' weel, Ma.'

'Whit's rang wi ye?'

'Ah've got a sair belly.'

'Ye gie me a sair belly! Better stay whur y'are then. Ah'm awa' tae the launderette. See ye later.'

Billy slept dreamlessly for what seemed like hours. It was in fact eleven when he woke and left his room in search of fodder. There was half a sliced loaf in the cupboard. He examined it, fetched the knife from his chest, cut off the bluc bits and toasted scveral slices. The milk was off so he made do with a cup of black Nescafé. The toast burnt, he scraped it in the sink and found some spread in the fridge. Taking his breakfast to the sitting room, he cleared enough debris to sit on the sofa and turned the TV on. He was still there when his mum came back around three.

'Ye could o' cleaned the place up!'

She struggled round the door with two plastic bags of shopping from Asda.

'Git aff yer arse and help me!'

He took the bags into the kitchen and unpacked them. Four bottles of white wine, a loaf, two tins of baked beans, one with sausages, half a dozen eggs, processed cheese slices, and a bag of potatoes. His mum collapsed on her chair.

'Ye can make yersel' some beans, if yer belly's better,' she said sarcastically.

'D'ye want some?'

'Noo.'

'Ye should eat.'

'Who's tellin' me wha' to doo? Anyway Ah had a pie at The Croone.'

Billy made his meal and carried it to his place on the settee. His mother had the remote and was flicking through shopping channels.

'Th' newsagents on th' Mall waz dun ower again.'

'Waz it? How d'ye ken?'

'They wur talkin' aboot it in tha laundry. Bastarts trussed him up in tin-foil, like a fookin' turkey… Ye dinnae seem very interested. He waz a guid feller, Mr Hussein. Always gave ye a bit o' tick if ye waz short…'

'How is he?'

'Who?'

'Mr Hussein, av coorse.'

'He's deed! Stabbed him in the neck, the bastarts… Are ye gan to gie me a bloody drink or wha'?'

Mr Elder was scratching numbers on the board and talking at the same time. Billy, somewhere in the middle of the classroom, was not paying attention. He had shaved his head earlier. His mother had screamed when he'd come out of the bathroom.

'Wha' the fook 'av ye done?'

He looked pathetic, skinnier than usual, in his pyjama bottoms. 'Yer no' gan oot like tha.'

Billy pushed past her and pulled on his school clothes.

'They'll no' recognise ye! Hav yer got a hat?'

She opened a cupboard, rummaged through and produced two — a flat hat belonging to some long-ago caller, and a woolly hat with a tassel. It was pink.

He'd taken the flak on the school bus.

'Yer big jessie … Billy bumboy.'

'A pink fairy-cake!' It was good-humoured enough.

'Right, you can use your calculators, I want an answer to that in ten minutes.'

Mr Elder stepped away. Billy looked at the equation that covered the whole width of the board. He knew the answer:

$p = 0.0016$. He fiddled about with his calculator, he had to appear to be working it out or he'd be accused of cheating. At one point in his school life he believed that working it through in his head was cheating. He'd taken beatings for it. He started to work out the formula for the probability of Callum and his henchman finding him. He didn't hear Mr Elder asking for the answer. Several hands had gone up, all answering hopefully but none correctly. He jumped as he heard his name bellowed.

'And what is so fascinating in the playground, Billy Logan? And since when have woolly hats been allowed in the classroom?'

'He's gan bald, Sir.'

'Be that as it may, would you happen to know the answer to the equation on the board?'

Billy would often give a wrong answer. Sticking one's head above the parapet was not wise in St Cuthbert's High School.

'P = 0.0016, Sir.'

'That is correct. Clearly the woolly hat has a beneficial effect on the brain — you have permission to wear it in my class.'

'Thank you, Sir.'

With each day that passed Billy felt less frightened. Reason said that 'they' could not possibly know that he had followed them into the shop. He heard nothing more about it. If it had made the local news he had missed it; these sorts of casual murders had long ceased to make headlines. By Friday, his head itched so much he left his hat off and resolved to let his hair grow again. It was Club night, and Mark called for him after his tea.

They found a burst football in the park with enough air left for a bit of a boot. They dribbled and passed it down the tunnel and lost it at the end, down a bank.

'Did ye hear aboot auld Hussein?' Mark asked as they passed his closed shop.

'Aye.'

'Poor auld bastart.'

Music was blaring out from the hall windows. It wouldn't be long before old Ivan would be down, banging on the door with his stick.

'Wha's on?' Billy asked

'Wretch 32, int it?'

'"Doing OK"?'

'Nah, the noo wan.'

Inside, at the other end of the hall from the table tennis and pool table, Hugh was with a small group looking at maps. He had his laptop open and the boys had compasses — he was teaching navigation. This was the final of six classes, in preparation for a field trip next week when the school holidays began. Mark and Billy joined the group.

'Youse live the nearest an y'are always late.'

'Sorry, Hugh. Ma maw was late back.'

'Aye, right.'

The usual excuse. Hugh dismissed it, though it was probably true. They knew Billy's situation. 'Hae ye got yer compass?'

'Aye.' Billy searched his pockets and found it. They were plotting a hike in Campsie Fells. Billy worked with Mark, and despite their being late they were the first to complete. They had to wait for the others so they wandered off to try and muscle in on a game of pool.

'Whur's Ken t'night?' Bill asked Wesley at the pool table.

'He's in the back wi the polis.'

'Wha's tha' aw aboot?' Wesley shrugged.

Billy moved off to where he could see through an internal window into the office where Ken was sitting with two uniformed policemen. He walked past and glanced in. On the desk was a grey tracksuit jacket. Billy (obsessed latterly with probabilities) knew without calculation that it was his, the one he ineffectively covered the old man with. At that moment Ken got up, and the policemen followed him out; Billy was behind the door as they came through. Ken unlocked the main door for them to leave.

'Turn the player down a wee bit, Ken. We've had complaints.'

'Ivan?'

'Aye.'

'OK, an Ah'll gie ye a bell later on.'

Ken turned the player right off. The silence was startling, and long enough for Ken to call the boys together. They sensed that this was more than a discussion of activities.

'Ye'll be wonderin' what tha' waz aw aboot.' The boys were rapt. 'Ye ken tha' Mr Hussein from the paper shop was murdered last week… Weel, it seems tha' wan o' youse waz in th' shop when it happened, or right efter.'

There were whistles, whether of shock or excitement the boys themselves didn't know.

'Is tha' right, Ken?'

'Wha' they telt youse?'

'How d'ye ken?''

'Never bin in the place.'

'They want tae peen it on us!'

'Hang on, boys. They dinnae want to pin it on any of youse. They're not accusin' you. They're lookin' fur a witness.'

'Well they can fook aff and look samwhur else.'

'Why are they sae sure it was wan of us?'

'Whoever it was used his jacket to cover Mr Hussein up and it had a boys' club membership card in the pocket.'

'Who is it, Sir?'

The gravity of the situation called for the formal address.

Throughout all this Billy was silent and — apart from his acned face looking a slightly brighter red — showed no emotion.

'Hiy Ken, does th' witness get poot up in a posh place an' fed smoked salmon an' steaks ta keep 'im safe? Cuz if so, it waz me,' Wesley said.

'No, it wasnae. Ye wur shaggin' ma sister. It waz me Ken, honest.'

'Quit it,' Ken said. 'This is serious and Ah expect better of youse. Ah'm in the office so Ah expect whoever it waz in tha' shop tae come an' explain themselves tae me before we close up. Awright?'

The navigation crew gathered around Hugh, asking questions that he would not or could not answer, so attention gradually returned to the hike they were planning for next Friday. Various routes had been drawn and distances calculated. From these a master route was decided on and the boys then had to describe the course as clearly as possible so it could be followed by a non-map-reader. By nine-thirty the work was done and the tables began to be cleared. No one had visited the office. Hugh gathered everyone and gave instructions to those who were going on the hike about where to gather for the van pick-up.

'And we'll have a visitor with us. Some o' ye who waz in the Hebrides at Easter will remember Derek who came kayaking wi' us, and stayed around for a couple of days.' No one seemed to remember. 'Och, weel mebbe when you see him. Stick together lads on the way home.'

The boys gathered any stuff they had and shambled out the door. Billy hung back.

'Are ye no' comin' Bill?' Mark called. Billy didn't move.

'Och, Christ, it waz you.' Billy tuned his back and went into the office.

Ken went with him to the police station. They waited in a queue to talk to the woman behind the counter, and then waited in the waiting area, to be called through. Billy was hyped-up, edgy, Ken couldn't get him to sit still. He read all the notices and talked loudly to Ken about them.

'Parking regulations — boring. Drink driving — is tha' real Ken, or did they make it up? They couldnae tell th' ambulance tae wait while they took th' photy. Mebbe they did, mebbe they added mair fake bluid.' He moved on.

'Dangerous Dogs Act — there's wan o' them in oor flats. Nasty bastart — calls it Satan. Ah'd like tae pish on th' manky shite.'

'Wheesht, Billy. Tha's enough now.'

'Ah should tell on him while Ah'm here. He's no allowed it in the flats.'

'Sit down, Billy.'

A woman came in with her face all battered, and started screaming about her old man.

'Look at ma face, ma bloody guidman done it. Bloody pished!'

The counter woman rang a bell and a couple of police constables hustled her out. A door at the back opened and Billy's name was called.

'DI Munroe.' He held out his hand and Ken shook it. 'Are you his faither?'

Ken explained who he was and that Billy lived with his mum, but she'd asked him to come with him. They'd get the picture. They were taken through to an interview room. Ken was allowed to sit at the back with a uniformed policeman, while Billy faced two plain-clothes officers across a table.

'You were in the shop the night Mr Hussein was killed?'

'Aye, and Ah ken who did it.'

'How do you know who did it?'

'It waz the same cunts who stole ma keks an'' took ma medal.'

Billy went through the whole story of his mugging and how he'd followed the pair the next night, about how long they were in the shop, and about what he'd found. His fear was allayed by his prominent role as saviour and chief witness.

'He wasnae deed then, jus' bleedin.'

'And was it you who covered him up?'

'Aye, wi tin-foil. We did first aid at Club, wi Ken.'

He looked over his shoulder.

'Hypothermia cuz of shock, see. Sorry it didnae work though.'

'Could you describe these men?' Billy saw that face leering towards him in the tunnel again.

'Aye, Ah could — wan o' them anyway. The other wan's cawd Callum.'

'Callum, are you sure?'

'Av coorse Ah'm shair.'

A weekend to sort himself out was now entering its third week, and although he was on his own, apart from the cats, his sister had made it quite clear he was to have made other arrangements by the time they got home from their caravan holiday in North Wales. He'd applied for a post as English teacher in a sixth form college in Stoke-on-Trent, but had been turned down. What had previously seemed like a marvellous release, a time of change and rejuvenation, was slipping into mid-life gloom. The summer was sneaking away. He brooded on what had happened at St Edmund's and was alternately furious and wounded.

His sister and her husband lived in a small house in Edgbaston. She was a librarian at the university and her husband Ron worked for the MG Rover group (now Chinese owned) and was in constant fear of redundancy. It was not an atmosphere conducive to liberated creativity. It was a relief when they went away. Derek spent time each day wandering in the local park. He carried a book but never opened it. Depression was doing its evil work. Regular dog walkers began to nod at him as they passed, he must be becoming a fixture.

The day was without weather: grey, but neither pale, promising sun, nor purplish and brooding; just grey. There was no wind, though the sycamore leaves wobbled slightly. It was dry-ish, or wet-ish, depending on your point of view. State school holidays had just begun so the park was more populated than previously. He could hear the whoops from the boating lake, ice cream vans had appeared. Should he buy one? No, not on his own; cornets were for children and young lovers.

The Arts Centre in the park had an exhibition of pottery, but he couldn't be bothered. He continued round the two-kilometre route. Breaking from his daily routine, he stepped off the main path and followed a trail to a small Japanese garden, a tiny area with two standing stones in a sea of gravel enclosed by maples. There were very un-Japanese weeds among the gravel. It had been created in the sixties when such design was innovative. Now it just looked a little sad, unloved and inappropriate. Bit like himself, he thought.

He lingered. A young couple joined him, and sat on a stone bench at one end of the gravel plot; he sat opposite them on an identical bench. She wore a long brightly coloured skirt and a skimpy top, he was in shorts and T-shirt. Derek was in denim jeans with a formal shirt and lace-up shoes. The couple ignored him as they produced a spliff and shared it between them. They both wore headphones and their heads nodded in unison. The smell of marijuana drifted across, producing memories of student days long gone. Derek raised two fingers in a sign of peace. There was no response, perhaps they hadn't seen or — more likely — that was then, this was now. He felt foolish. The girl lay along the bench with her head in her boyfriend's lap.

Was Derek intruding? He was rooted to his bench and had stayed long enough to feel that leaving would be a censure, a condemnation even, of the couple's behaviour. He moulded with the stone, became a part of the garden. There was a sound — he hadn't noticed it before, trickling water from a stream — that transported him to Chris's garden, and Max, smells from the spliff superimposed by the smell of roses. The water became the sea as he sat on rocks near the school and then in the Hebrides, breaking waves and seaweed, and the weed in the tent, and the stars above and such laughter. The couple were walking towards him. Derek stood. The young woman was very tall, he had not noticed that before. They came closer and to his astonishment she stood in front of him and kissed him on the forehead, then she stepped aside and the young man hugged him. Wordlessly they left the way they had come.

Derek left too, and stopped on the way back to buy an ice cream.

He walked along the avenue of seventies semis, with their neat front gardens reflecting the owners' taste: gravel with succulents, clipped box, low shrubs and heathers, roses and cottage style. The houses had replacement windows, lined curtains, freshly painted front doors. Maybe, just maybe, this could have been his life with Chris, but not now, so not now. He made a cup of tea and headed into the garage. The garage was a store, the car stood outside. He started to unpack, select his immediate future, and repack. Books in boxes stayed, all items of furniture (not many, all there was) stayed. Warm clothes, rucksacks, hiking boots, climbing equipment, a tent, primus stove, bedding, all transferred to the boot of his car.

How grateful, how indebted, he felt towards the Japanese garden couple.

He worked through a list, cancelling his viewings of studio flats, asking the neighbours to take over feeding the cats, cleaning his room and the kitchen. Packing for his immediate needs.

Finally, he opened his laptop. He hadn't emailed Ken, he wouldn't email Ken; he was going anyway so there would be time enough to call when he was in Glasgow. He didn't look online for teaching posts north of the border; he was going anyway. He'd find his feet when he was there. He checked a site for rented accommodation. He'd be OK. He booked a small hotel for five nights. Wow, such energy. During a quick scan of the mainly spam emails his eyes caught max@henderson.com.

Dear Derek,

Please forgive me for writing to you, I know you think it best if we don't communicate but you asked me to write my experiences in Argentina during the Easter holiday. Well I've attached a short essay. You will know when you read it that I will not be going back there, whatever they say. I never want to glimpse that foul man again. I don't know what my mother sees in him. And if she marries him I'm still not going. I blame him for the things that happened at the end of last term.

As you are no longer at the school surely there is no reason why we can't talk, email, or even meet occasionally. I feel that you understood me in a way that nobody else does. I don't know anyone else I can talk to about things. I persuaded Monica to give me your email, she is a bit of a softie. I'm spending the Summer with my father, he is getting married again but I haven't met his fiancée yet. He's got a new boat so we will be going sailing, I'll probably be sick.

I hope you like my essay, do write back.

With sincere admiration,

Max

He read the essay. It was a well-constructed, amusing piece about a gay boy in macho-land. Monica a softie? Like a tarantula's a softie!

Ina Logan, born in Glasgow, mother, diabetic, one son, fourteen, father unknown, watched the world go round in the form of her dirty clothes in the biggest machine in the launderette — the launderette that never closed. She could have done her washing at two or three or four o'clock, but it was in fact eight o'clock and Mary (who did custom washes during the daylight hours) would be in soon.

Ina busied herself, wiping the spilt powder and gathering up all the odd socks, knickers and other small garments left behind by customers; they never came back for them, people didn't used to be so wasteful.

The shop had a noticeboard; 'Armchair for sale, very comfy'; 'Puppies free to a good home;' 'Housework help, references supplied'. Mary charged two pounds a week per notice, but they never got taken down. When Ina was satisfied that the shop was spick and span, she produced the photograph from her bag, and pinned it in the centre of the board. She stepped back to see its effect, cleared a few old notices that surrounded it and was satisfied.

Mary struggled through the door with two bags with at least twenty kilos of washing in each. 'Guid mornin' Ina. Not like youse to be sae early.'

'Och weel, the lad's aff skool so Ah've nothin' tae do.'

'It'll be a wee while till The Crowne opens.'

'Ah may not go today. Ah've got some notices tae put up.'

'Och aye, waz tha' aboot then?' Mary was sorting her bags of laundry into cool wash, hot wash, delicates, heavy soil etcetera.

'Haen't ye seen this?'

'Whit's tha'?'

Ina pointed to the noticeboard.

'Who put tha' there? Bloody "Crimestoppers", they can pay their two quid like anyone else. Ugly bastart, wha's he meant tae have done then?' Mary went closer. 'Forgot mah bloody glasses agin.'

She peered at the writing. 'Aboot auld Hussein, eh? Poor auld bastart.'

Ina would have preferred it if there were more people in the shop but she was bursting and couldn't stop herself.

'Ma lad did tha.'

'Yer wha'?'

'Billy.'

'Billy did in auld Hussein?'

'Nah, yer bampot, he did the picture, he waz there, see?'

A black chap came in with his washing.

'Can youse dae this fer me?'

'Ay sunshine, put it at the back, payment on collection. Let's git this straight, yer Billy were a witness.'

'Aye, he waz there.'

'He wasnae.'

'He waz there, and this polis fella came round and they done this picture.'

'Weel, tha's somethin', innit.'

Mary went back to sorting her washing and Ina, triumphant, moved her clothes to the dryer. Every customer who ventured in with their washing, or who just called for a gossip, had their attention drawn to the noticeboard — 'Best be on the look-oot fer tha' hairy bastard who done in auld Hussein, ma Billy's a witness' — and the like, till Ina felt it time to do her civic duty and spread the word at the social, the labour club, the doctor's, the footie park, and finally at The Crowne.

Derek sat at the bar, above which a notice read:

'WATCH HERE, FOOTBALL, RUGBY, F1, GAELIC FOOTBALL, HURLING.'

His beer was served by a young woman whose accent was so thick he could hardly understand her. He'd smiled as she served him his pint and later worked out that she'd said, 'What's a nice young man like you doing in a place like this?' He smiled again. He was not young, at forty-six, going bald and grey, but for the last week he had felt young again. It was early evening and there were plenty of drinkers in the bar and the booths. The music was Country and Western, maudlin. A woman, the worse for drink, lurched to the fruit machine, fed it and cursed, as the lights spun and settled, with no comforting concluding jingle of coins.

'Ah fook! Gie us another white wine, Hen!'

The barmaid poured a third of a bottle into a glass and took her money. The woman returned to her seat, unsteady, but without spilling a drop.

'Derek, ma man, guid to see youse.'

He looked up. There was Ken, as he remembered him; short, round, self-assured, buoyant, with those inimitable eyebrows. They shook hands.

'What can Ah get ye?'

Derek said he was OK, Ken got himself a half pint and they moved to a booth.

'Well man, what brings ye to this part of the world?'

'Relocating.'

'Ah can think of better places on the planet than Cumbernauld.'

Those eyes penetrated as they had on Barra. Derek told his story; the school that he felt out of place in, the boy he'd befriended, the bastard Head, the toadying staff, the play, the incident, the resignation. He told Ken everything — except that Chris had betrayed him. That his own private pain.

'That's a sorry tale, Derek, but I cannae see why it's brought you up here.' You, Derek wanted to say — your inspiration brought me here.

'Something different, something more real, education to change lives.'

'That's a bit idealistic, young man.'

Young man again. Derek smiled.

'Maybe, but I've found a studio flat in Glasgow to give me time to look around. Meanwhile I wondered if you could use any help with the club?'

'Aye, Ah can always do with some help. We've been teaching them navigation and we're taking a group up to Campsie fells at the weekend. That's your kind o' stuff, Ah reckon.'

Derek eagerly agreed that it was. The pub was filling up: the few who had jobs coming in after work — prey for the rest who survived on hand-outs.

'Hey, hey, youse at the bar,' the fruit machine woman shouted. 'Gie us a drink, there's a honey.' A bloke looked round.

'A white wine is it, Hen?'

'Youse a darlin'. A darlin'. Come ower 'ere, Ah's got a story fer ye.'

He took her a drink, saying he was going outside for a cig.

'Gie us a ciggie too, an Ah'll tell youse a story.'

She followed him out of the pub to the tiny boarded-off yard that advertised itself as 'The Beer Garden'. It was an apt description, as nothing else grew there; her beau tipped a full ashtray, swimming in nicotine brine from an earlier rain shower, into a flower pot containing a barely breathing hydrangea.

'Ah've not seen youse here before.'

He rolled her a ciggie.

'D'ye no' have a proper wan?' she said disdainful of his offer.

'You'll be wantin' the crown jewels next.'

'Giz it here then.'

She stumbled closer to him for a light.

'Tha's a guid wan.'

'Eh?'

'The crown jewels…this is the bloody Crown — get it? Yer not from round here.'

With someone to listen to her, Ina began her story for the umpteenth time, now lacking its original passion, but making up for it in sentiment, embellished by many repetitions. The gang of five, with crowbars and hammers, held at bay 'fer haff an ooer' by the skill and bravery of young Billy. 'Ma wee boy, like David against a fookin' Goliath'.

Others had come out to smoke. With another audience, the loop continued. 'Gie's a drink and Ah'll tell youse a true story…'

Derek and Ken were on their second drink when the football started, and the two men, comfortable with each other, settled down to watch. Suddenly, above the sound of the television, came screaming and shouting of a different order. The outside door crashed open and a couple came in.

'There's a mad woman oot there — she needs locking up.'

The landlord moved fast from behind the bar and collided with Ken heading in the same direction. A loud crash came from outside, as a table was turned over and glass shattered everywhere.

'That's it! Y'ar pished and a bloody mad woman, yer drivin' ma customers away. Ah'm callin' the polis, and yer never to set foot in here again.' Ina turned from among the debris and blinked as though the chaos that surrounded her had appeared as an act of God.

'Hang on there Joey, no need fer the polis, I'll see to her,' Ken said.

'She's callin' me a fookin' liar, she's the fookin' liar, ma son waz there.'

'OK Ina, time to go home now.'

Ken caught hold of her, firmly though not inconsiderately, and took her through the pub and onto the street and — so as not to lose his grip on Ina — asked Derek to call a taxi. Ina mumbled on, contradicting herself and speaking gibberish, until the taxi arrived. Ken shoved her in and gave the taxi driver the address and the fare. He leaned through the window.

'Ye should try and keep yer mouth shut Ina, ye never know who's listening.'

She slurred something inaudible, probably 'fuck off', and the taxi pulled away.

'She's a bit the worse for wear. Are you always such a Good Samaritan?'

'Ah know her son.'

'Well, she's lucky not to be spending the night in a cell.'

'You know her son too.'

'Do I?'

'Billy. In your kayak gang at Easter. Let's have another and Ah'll tell youse all aboot him.'

The minibus was due to leave Cumbernald at eight-fifteen on Saturday morning. Derek caught an early train from Glasgow feeling great. This was real work, somewhere to make a difference. There were rain clouds about — usual for this part of the world, even in August. Across the car park he waved at Hugh who was having a quick smoke before boarding.

'Good morning, Hugh.'

'Derek, guid to see you again, man. Ken said you were visiting. How are you doing?'

'Not bad, looking forward to today.'

He didn't know how much Ken had told him. Boys began to arrive.

'Can we get on the bus Hugh? I wannae sit in the back.'

'Youse can wait for Ken, ye know the rules.'

An ancient black Golf pulled into the car park. Ken got out, clipboard in hand, and counted the twelve boys. He had a boot full of lunch packs, small backpacks for those who needed them, compasses for those who had forgotten, and boots for the inappropriately shod.

'It's gan tae be boggy, ye no' wearin' trainers.'

Derek remembered the humour and character of the boys as they shoved and elbowed to get their lunch packs. Billy was at the back. He seemed taller and skinnier than at Easter. His crew-cut didn't disguise several angry pustules on his forehead.

He looked bothered. Derek decided to find an opportunity to talk to him.

With Hugh driving they set off at around eight-forty-five. Ken stood up to give instructions, his squat figure balancing securely between the rows of seats.

'OK now. The plan is to go a bit further into the hills today. It's a longer hike than we've done before, twenty-five kilometres.'

'Tha's like walkin' tae bloody Glasgae!'

There were semi-serious groans from the lads who nevertheless appeared excited by the prospect.

'You will be navigating yourselves in your small groups.'

'Kin we have oour dinner now, Ken.'

'Definitely not. Ye'll need to eat on the walk. Another thing the group will have to decide is when tae take breaks.'

'Kin we git some chips on the way?'

Ken pulled paper bags from his rucksack and gave every lad a bacon roll.

'You think of everything.' Derek said.

'Some of them won't hae had any breakfast. Tha's nae way tae set oot on a five-hour hike. How about yoursel?'

'Well it was a long time ago.'

'I bought yer one in case.'

The bus stop-started its way through the outskirts of Cumbernauld, where many of the shops were boarded up, due to closure or against crime. The bookmakers and the pound shops were clearly advertised. A last set of lights and without warning the countryside began — farmland, with hills in the distance. They'd been in the bus about an hour when Ken pointed out the escarpment of the Fintry and Gargunnock hills. The boys would be divided into three groups of four, and there would be one adult with each group. Derek would set off with his group first, Ken following fifteen minutes later. Hugh would then drive back for half a mile to park the bus, and set off with his group, walking first along the road, fifteen minutes after Ken. They expected to rendezvous back at the bus sometime between three and four p.m.

Ken read out the names of the first group. 'Billy, Mark, Wesley and Ian — youse are to go with Derek. Billy and Wesley are in charge of the route to the top of Carleatheran. Ye'll know ye there when ye reach the burial chamber, then Ian and Mark take over navigation'

'Whit's he do, eh?' Wesley said, indicating Derek.

'He enjoys the view. Now get on your way.'

It was nearly half past ten and colder than it had been in the city. Darker clouds were welling behind the hills. Derek was confident that Ken had prepared them for all weathers. They set off on a farm track. It was dry and easy walking and the boys made a good pace.

'Ah think we should decide when tae have ower dinner, like Ken said.' Ian was always hungry.

'It's only ten o'clock.'

'Weel Ah'm gan tae have ma Lucozade.'

'Fine but you'll no' get mine later.' Mark said.

Billy looked at his map,

'We'll cross the Boquan Burn soon, youse can have a drink there.'

'Is that a café?'

'No yer great diddy, it's a stream.'

'Ah'm no' drinking from a burn, coows shite in it.'

And the chat and the banter continued and included Derek with more and more familiarity as they progressed.

Breaks in the cloud illuminated the escarpment like a dramatic backcloth; a large bird sat on a fence post in front of them.

'Look at tha,' Ian said. 'Tha's a big fooker.'

The bird took off in ungainly fashion and beat its great wings in slow motion.

'Tha's a fookin eagle! Tha's an eagle, in't it, Derek?'

'No, a buzzard, look at the white underneath its wings.'

The bird soared higher and was joined by another. Boys craned their heads, gasped at the wheeling performance.

'They sound like my ma's cat in th' alley.'

'Whit dae they eat?'

'Mice and rats and stuff.'

'They'd be welcome at our flats then.'

They were quite close to a farm entrance now and Wesley decided it was time to look at their maps and get their bearings with a compass.

'Nah, we kin see the way, we're heading for that break up there, cuz we're nae going ower the top.'

'OK clever dick, and wha 'appens when we're in a bog, or we lose our way, and tha' fookin' greet cloud spews up.' Wesley was concerned about safety, Mark and Ian resented his leadership, Billy was quiet, but helped him with the map.

'Ah could've telt youse it waz this way.'

They continued towards the farm, before taking a side turning, still on a track and slowly rising. When they were up above the farm Wesley insisted that they leave the track and take a less trodden grassy way, still rising. There was a reluctance to follow his instructions. They hung around for a bit, quarrelling.

'Come on man, we dinnae want th' others tae catch up.'

Derek resolved the issue as diplomatically as possible and they followed Wesley's route. On this steady climb, Billy hung back and Derek walked alongside him.

'I hear you were awarded a medal, Billy, for the trip to the Hebrides.'

'Aye, but some murderin' bastart stole it.'

Derek regretted his opening gambit, he wanted to get Billy's mind away from his problems. The boy was not how Derek remembered him, a young Launcelot Gobbo taking on the world with his conscience. The boy who walked beside him was hard, defensive and morose. He was fourteen years old, too small, malnourished. Maybe his father had been a boxing lightweight who once won a bout, but Billy wouldn't go a round.

'Do you have any brothers or sisters, Billy?'

'Nah.' The boy was giving no help.

'Just you and your mum then?'

'And me nan.'

There was no opportunity for further conversation as the ground became extremely boggy and they had to find their individual best routes. Mark was swearing over to the left as his one of his boots became submerged. The group struggled on, alternately cursing their plight, and enjoying the misfortunes others encountered. They gathered again near the top where their route ran much closer to the escarpment. Billy joined Derek once again.

'We're nearly a' the top aff Carleathean, tha's 485 metres. Stronend is the next highest point, hill number 1659, OS grid reference is 62927 89472, 511 metres, or 1,677 feet.' Derek turned to look at 'this wee boy' as Ken called him.

'Did you learn all that for the trip?'

'Nah, read it on th' map on th' way up.'

'And remembered it?' Derek was astonished.

'Aye, Ah like numbers.'

'Is maths your favourite subject?'

'Aye, but Mr Elder disnae like me.'

'Why is that, do you think?'

'Ah can work it oot faster than he can.'

'Would you like to do maths at university?'

'Univairsity?'

'Yes.'

'If Ah'm lucky I'll get a job next year in the food processin' factory. If no', it's the dole.'

'It needn't be like that.'

'Yer a fookin eejit.'

Billy ran ahead to join the other lads who were now approaching the trig point at the top of Carleatheran.

Derek was rightly scolded. He recognised his innocence and ignorance and resolved to watch without interference. He trailed after the boys, big boys, men's voices, except Billy? The final mound was stony and uneven. He kept his eyes down and watched his step, his hiking pole glanced off fragmenting granite, he almost expected sparks. At the top he raised his head to the view, there were no boys to be seen. He scanned three-sixty degrees. The burial chamber was situated fifteen yards away. Beyond it, incongruously, was a wind farm. The chamber was little more than a circle of fallen walls, though there must have been a way into the mound to carry in the dead. A wife or a husband or a whole family perhaps. A strange roaring came from inside the walls. He guessed that was where they'd be. Wesley's head popped over the wall.

'The yeti's got me. Help, Derek, help.'

The roar turned to hilarity as Derek approached.

'Where youse bin, man? Ah thought ye waz good at this hiking lark!'

The boys were sitting round on stones, their backs to the prevailing wind, shielded by the walls, unpacking their lunches.

'It's bleedin' brown bread.'

'Swap ye an apple fer yer sarnie.'

'Fook off, bampot.' Ian started coughing.

'Ah swallied a top.' Derek moved quick and thumped his back.

'Tha's right, puke it up, Ian man.' Ian did and the offending top of a fizzy drink lay on the ground.

'Whit yer do that fer? It's not a bleedin' dummy.'

'Time for a group photo.' Derek fumbled for his mobile.

'Have ye got a series six?' someone asked. Wesley looked over.

'Nah it isnae. Tha's rubbish tha.'

'Well it takes good picture so gather in.' After much pushing and shoving, the picture was posed.

'Where's Billy?' Derek asked.

They looked around and shouted.

'He'll av gone for a pish.'

They stood on the walls of the burial chamber and wobbled on the rocks, shouted and fell off.

'Maybe he's gan fer a jobby!' Much hilarity. 'He'll be back.'

Derek looked beyond the walls. Despite the gathering intensity of the cloud mass, he could see a mile or so in all directions; a boy, even as slight as Billy, would be visible. Rain was inevitable. Derek drew his waterproof from his pack.

'Did Billy tell anyone he was going?' The boys were unconcerned and continued tidying everything back into their packs as they finished.

'Ah'm going fer a pish,' announced Mark. 'Dinna come round this side.'

'Are ye frightened we might see yer dobber?' Mark went behind the stone wall.

Billy had been gone ten minutes, maybe more. The three boys started to scan the land around them.

'Has he got a phone?' Derek asked.

'Yeah, he had my old one, but he's never got credit,' Wesley said.

They tried it nevertheless but it was out of service. Derek had to do something, the boys were making up wilder and wilder stories about where he could be. He suggested they cover ground in all directions, calling for no longer than five minutes, and then return to the lunch spot. Derek took the way they had come.

From the escarpment Derek could see Ken and his gang in the boggy ground below. The curses and shouts reached him incoherently, like the school playing field from the quiet of his flat. Derek ran, careless of the ground. He had to tell Ken. Ken would know what to do.

'Hae ye got a problem?' Derek explained. 'How long?'

'Maybe twenty minutes by now, if he's not back.'

Ken shouted at his boys to keep up and set off at a fast walk towards the top, asking no more questions. Derek struggled to keep up.

Billy was not there when they arrived. Ken interrogated the boys who had been searching, what was the terrain? Any footprints? Places to hide? What was his mood like on the walk?

'He waz a bit crabbit, kept talkin' numbers, like when he's bothered.'

'Who saw him last?'

Ian said 'He waz wi Derek there, we waz in front and reached this place. Then Billy jumped in and said we should crouch and roar to frighten Derek.'

'An did ye do that?'

'Aye.'

'And after that?'

'I dinna know.'

'Stay here, all of youse. Ah'm going to look round.' Ken set off, examining the ground in ever-increasing circles around the walls of the burial chamber. Derek moved away, not to be engaged in the speculation of the seven boys now together, and engaging in the drama. The wind, which was bringing the rain, flapped at his jacket. He zipped it up and felt the first spots.

Ken returned after a while, talking on the phone to Hugh. The boys, with the exception of Wesley, were to retrace the way they had come till they met Hugh's party, then they were all to return to the bus and be taken home. Wesley and Derek were to stay and wait for instructions from the police and Mountain Rescue team. Grumbling, wanting to be part of 'search and rescue', they set off with a big lad from Ken's group in charge. Ken then made the necessary calls to the authorities.

'Yer fookin' eejit.'

'Git down youse lot, give the bampot a fright.'

Ian let out a bloodthirsty yowl, learnt from *Horrors of the Dark Pit* and perfected over many weeks; the others hunkered down and howled like wolves.

Billy slipped out of the chamber on the opposite side and sprinted over the rough terrain. Billy could run, his feet skimming the surface, leaving tumbles of small rock slides in his wake.

He reckoned he had a minute, maybe two, to reach the nearest of the grouse-butts that littered the moorland. This terrain, taken at speed, might have twisted the ankle of a heavier boy but Billy made it, hardly even breathless. The butt, built like a wooden urinal, was roofless. The gun slit faced away from the hilltop so he had no way of knowing if anyone was looking for him. He listened attentively; they would be bound to call soon. The line of butts stretched away on the side of the hill, about thirty metres apart. Next week the hill would explode with gunshot and small corpses, but Billy didn't know about that.

It was getting prematurely dark. This would help. Too bad his waterproof was gleaming yellow. They wouldn't catch quite so many grouse if they were like fucking canaries, Billy thought. As though on cue, a small brown bird, superbly camouflaged, strutted bravely by. It cracked its call. A buzzard whined above him. Billy darted, bent over, almost on all fours, using light hands as well as light feet, to reach the next butt. If he could make it to the following one he would be out of direct vision from the top, though any search would begin in the butts.

He reached the third one, now a little breathless and sat on the damp ground. In his pocket he reached for a crumpled piece of paper. A teenaged girl, a stranger in uniform jeans and hoodie, had shoved it into his hand as he'd left the flats this morning. She had run up to him and, whilst looking at the ground, she had grabbed his hand and put the note in it. Then she was gone round the corner of the flats towards the recycle yard.

He spread the note out. It was written on a sheet torn from a jotter.

We know where you live Billy Logan, you can't hide. Expect us soon you little snitching shit.

Far away and mixed with the whine of the buzzard, he heard his name being called. If he moved, he would be exposed on this barren hill.

The opening to the butt was a narrow slit. Opposite was a shelf below the look-out, where the hunters' guns would rest. He crept under the shelf in its darkest corner. Dark, damp, a mouse ran across his foot, he jumped and hit his head on the shelf. The calling was closer now. He could hear Ian's voice. He was invisible, a bundle of sacks forgotten from last year's shooting. Closer still, Ian was just outside; then there was another voice, maybe Mark, further away.

'Away Ian man, time to go back.'

Scuffling noise, Ian was in the butt, then above his head. 'Billeeeee!' Movement. It was Ian leaving, and then nothing. After a minute Billy unravelled from his corner and looked out. He could just see the three friends converging. The rain was starting.

The police arrived first, two of them, leaving their vehicle where the track ended. They scrambled up the side of the escarpment where Ken, Derek and Wesley, were waiting. Shrinking visibility would hamper the search. The police said Mountain Rescue were on their way, with a dog handler. Ken had arranged for Hugh to return, after dropping the boys with some clothing of Billy's as a scent for the dog. A helicopter was on standby.

The rain blew across the terrain in waves. Ken, Derek and Wesley sheltered silently, hunkered down inside the burial chamber. An hour had passed; another vehicle arrived down at the Farm. The dog, its handler and several volunteers set off up the hill.

Hugh banged on the door as hard as he could and shouted through the letter-box.

'Are you in there, Mrs Logan? Ah've got tae talk to ye aboot Billy.' He could definitely hear a television. He tried banging again. There was shuffling and finally Ina's voice.

'Hush yer banging, gie a person time.'

Several bolts were pulled back, a chain left on, and Ina peered round. It was about one-thirty in the afternoon and she had on her nightie and dressing gown.

'Mrs Logan, my name's Hugh. I work with Ken at the Boys' Club. We took the lads up hiking on Campsie Fells this morning.'

'Ah know tha'. Whit's up?'

'Weel, it seems Billy took off, and there's a search party out after him.'

'Ma Billy! Ma Billy wouldnae do tha'. Youse best come in, sorry aboot the mess. Ah've not been too well.'

'I need to take something of Billy's, to let a dog sniff it, so we can find him.'

'Oh ma God! Ma Billy, ma wee boy.'

'It's all right, Mrs Logan, we'll find him, Ah just need tae drive back there as soon as possible with something of Billy's.'

Suddenly Ina connected.

'Wait there.' She went into a room and closed the door. there was much thudding as drawers and cupboards were opened and closed.

'Ah won't be a minute,' she called.

Five minutes later she appeared again, dressed, carrying a pair of pyjamas and a pillowcase.

'Ah'll just get ma keys.'

Hugh had not envisaged a passenger but did not stop to argue.

Two or three days maybe, Billy thought, till they thought he was dead and forgot about him. Then he could go to his nan's and maybe filch a loan and go south. He was hungry and sopping wet. His canary jacket (stupid fucking thing his mother got from the market) was still in his rucksack with his packed lunch. He'd save that till later, it would have to last him a while. His plan, such as it was, was to get off this hill and find a barn or a hut to hide in for a while. He couldn't go back the way he came, that was obvious. He struggled to read the map in the gloom of the butt, and on the gun ledge the rain soaked the paper. He pulled out his compass. If he retreated along the line of butts there was a track marked, heading north, that would take him towards the village of Gargunnock. But if he set off across-country he could pick up the path at the start of a burn. This would save him time, time he needed if a search began in earnest.

'Ah gotta git aff this fookin' hill and into some cover,' he said out loud.

The rain was steady, he was soaked already and cold. His rucksack was not waterproof; he ate a bar of chocolate he found inside his wet packet of sandwiches; he remembered making them at six-thirty that morning with the last of a loaf and some cheese slices, as his ma snored in the armchair. That was before. When he'd finished he put the wrapper in his pocket and set of at a slow jog, which slowed to a fast walk and then to a scramble as the terrain became more difficult. He looked round in the direction of Carleatheran from time to time but the trig point, and the hill itself, were invisible; he was alone on this desolate fell.

The ground had hidden rifts — some able to take a whole leg down to black water beneath; twice he'd fallen. He watched every step and tested the ground. Progress was slow. The weather made it impossible to check his compass direction against the map. He jumped across a particularly wide gap in the turf and heard running water beneath him. The burn was running out of sight. Confused, he considered retracing his path along the edge of the cleft as it might take him to a definite track. He began on this route, but after fifty metres changed his mind. Better to follow the water north; the ground, which had been falling, now levelled off and if he followed the water he must come to the edge, then if he turned to his right he could trail the top of the escarpment until it was low enough for him to clamber down.

Hugh pulled into the car park of the Gargunnock Inn. There were several police cars and some uniformed officers around.

'O ma God! Hae ye found ma Billy? Is he deed?' Hugh introduced Ina to an officer.

'No, Mrs Logan. I'm sure we'll find him. Have you brought some clothes for the scent?'

'Ye've got to find ma boy, ma lovely boy.' Ina was wailing again, it had been a difficult journey. A police 'off-road vehicle' sped out of the car park, taking Billy's pyjamas to the tracker dog.

'Is this a fookin' pub or wha?'

'Aye,' said Hugh, 'it is Hen. I'll buy you a drink.'

The dog was doing its job, nose to the ground, the onlookers stood waiting and hoping. It seemed the rain was hampering the scent trail. She went out and returned several times before she appeared sure and set off with her trainer on the end of a long leash. The rest followed some way behind. Progress was slow, not least because the dog lost the scent in places and doubled back to pick it up again. Her handler occasionally produced Billy's pyjamas from a plastic bag for her to sniff. Derek, though used to fell walking, slipped behind, the rain on his glasses added to the general lack of visibility. Ken indefatigable and as steadfast as the ancients, who brought their kings to be buried here, led the party behind the dog. A line of wooden huts emerged out of the mist ahead. Derek hurried, encouraged by the possibility of Billy sheltering in one of the butts, but his foot slipped into a rut and he was on the ground, his glasses gone, as the party, optimistic too at the sight of the butts made greater speed. Derek, on all fours, felt the sodden ground inch by inch. His glasses were his sight, precious since childhood, an extension of himself.

The dog chose a butt and was in and out in seconds, moving fast towards the next in line.

'He's been here,' the handler shouted back to Ken. At the next butt the dog spent longer, but as Ken and the others arrived she was nose to the ground again in line with the last one.

A member of the recue party fell back to find Derek.

'What's happened? Are you hurt?'

Derek explained and the woman scanned the ground.

'Here they are.' She picked them up. 'They're not damaged.' She pulled her scarf from inside her jacket and cleaned them for him.

'Here you are.'

Together they set off directly towards where the party had arrived at the last butt of the line.

'He's definitely been here.'

The dog sniffed around and was not keen to leave the corner where Billy had crouched.

'Look, a chocolate wrapper.'

Derek covered his disappointment at the lack of a shivering teenager crouched behind the entrance. The dog was off again, Derek went into the butt where Billy had been, it was like all the others, except for a small shelf that would have allowed better shelter. They'd found the wrapper there. Derek peered below the shelf. There was another scrap of something, maybe from his lunch. Head above the shelf, he reached down into the dank corner and felt around the wet earth for what his eyes had seen. Not a wrapper. He used his jacket to protect the writing from the rain, and read the note.

The forward party had slowed right down because of the rough terrain. The dog made many forays, only to return confused. Rain was now getting through jackets and into boots. Derek caught up with the major party that were now waiting for the dog. The sweat inside his clothes cooled and he shivered. He remembered Billy's clothes; thin jeans, T-shirt and cotton hooded jacket. Surely he would have a waterproof of sorts in his rucksack, Ken would have insisted. They were on a small incline now, heading towards the ridge, and it was clear to all that the dog had lost the scent. She made short forays, returning to look expectantly at her owner. He called her in and put her on a short lead.

'He was definitely in the butts, and maybe headed off in this direction but we can't be sure.'

The rescuers retraced their journey to the butts, following the line south to pick up a track that the shooting parties used. They then turned slightly north-west, following where it crossed the escarpment via a disused quarry. Once down, they were close to the village of Gargunnock, from where the rescue was being monitored. A helicopter was grounded in a field nearby. In the car park of the hotel, police and Mountain Rescue were in groups talking. It seemed impossible even for Ken to find out what was going on. Ken told Wesley that Hugh would take him home.

'No thanks. Ah want tae stay, Billy's ma mate.'

'What aboot your folks? They'll worry.'

'Och, dinnae fash yersel', Ah'll text them.' Ken said he could sleep in the van, but he'd speak to his mam first.

A large policeman came over. 'The helicopter is going up but he's not very hopeful in these conditions, says he'd be lucky to find a giraffe up there in this. But it's all we can do. We'll get more volunteers and start again at first light. The weather is going to be fine tomorrow.'

'Whit are ye going tae do, Derek?' Ken asked.

'I'll stay here.'

'Ye mustnae blame yersel'. Derek moved away so as not to embarrass himself as his eyes welled up.

'I'm going in to get dry, and sort myself a room.'

In the bar Ina had heard that the search had so far been unsuccessful. She was clinging to Hugh, red-eyed and quiet.

Billy was sodden; he had reached saturation; he was composed of water; but still the water came relentlessly on as though it could dissolve him into its own element. He was near the edge of the escarpment. There was a roaring, like thunder — a furious frightening roar. Water above and water below. He had no choice but to push blindly on. Fear in a tunnel, Billy knew. Not this. The water he had been following had gone underground, carving its way through rock as though it were soap. The noise was deafening. Billy gasped and fought until finally, close to the edge, he saw the power and ferocity of the pent-up element erupt: water gushed over the escarpment edge, and the descent produced a watershed-defying gravity, sending torrents upwards to meet the falling sheets; a rainbow god of water shimmered below him. In the battle of the elements, here was a victory.

Billy's heart sank. He was on the wrong side. To follow the route he had imagined for himself, he needed to be on the other side of the waterfall. He would have to go back to where the water went underground and approach from the other side. He would do it, it couldn't be far, and he believed the map and the clearly marked path off the ridge.

He didn't move immediately. He wanted to rest, and the magnificence of the sight held him in awe. He crouched and yelled in unison with the cataract, acknowledging its authority.

He crouched over his bag to get a dry shirt and the yellow waterproof. The dry shirt was damp, and more so by the time he had wrenched it over his head. The anorak was thin, but he felt better once it was zipped up. He swung the rucksack back over his shoulder and turned towards the moor, the way he had come. A shrub caught the strap of the bag and, in wrenching it away, he and the bag flew like a giant canary diagonally across the descending torrent. He flew through the rainbow with the dreadful noise of waters in his ears. Boann had taken her sacrifice.

The unrelenting roar engulfed him; he swung like a lead weight trying to find plumb. He reached above his head, downwards, and gripped a handful of gorse. It tore out of the rock as the force of his swing took him back, his head bouncing on bare rock like a tennis ball. His movement now reduced to a simple twist from left to right, the hand grabbing, like a dying man at his sheets, at anything solid. And still the waters roared in triumph.

The plane was indecipherable, the ground had tipped, a great force had turned the Earth through one-eighty degrees. His face sideways to the ground left one eye to scan the debris, the other forced into the talus. And so he hung, saw the helicopter but did not know its significance.

Something had caught him, and would not surrender. The natural order was inverted, feet where head should be. In his eyeline was bush, he squirmed his torso towards it and took hold steadily, bringing half his frame to a place of foundation.

He could turn and look up through dead branches into the deep grey. The rucksack had stuck close during his flight and now nestled in the spiny growth of the rock face, giving Billy a backrest. From where he half lay, he could see his legs wedged together between the trunk of a dead tree and the rock behind. He told his legs to move, and one responded; the other pointing upwards did not. Billy understood his situation.

In the bar of the Gargunnock Hotel the mood was sombre. A few locals stood quietly at one side of the bar. The rescue team had gone to their homes to prepare for an early start the following day. At a table Hugh, Ken, Derek, Wesley and Ina were silent. Derek wanted to show Ken the note he had found but thought that Ina might get hysterical; for now at least she was quiet. The note could wait. Wesley sipped coke and played games on his mobile phone. The men drank whisky. The landlord brought over a plate of sandwiches and would not take payment. They ate silently, connected only by their mental image of Billy somewhere on the fell, lost, injured, or worse? They went to bed early, arranging to meet at five a.m.

Billy saw a small bird on a branch above where his legs were twisted. It sang with a note that pierced the dull roar; a bird with a yellow breast that bobbed up and down and seemed curious about this strange creature below. Billy was grateful; it persuaded him he was alive. Slipping through collapsed time, he saw the bird, totally yellow and the size of a buzzard, scream at him. In his dream Billy controlled him, a master of ceremonies who placed for his trick three items: a dead rat, a cheese sandwich and his own leg. The bird was to swoop for each one in turn: on cue, to a drum roll, the bird seized the rat and flew up with it in its great beak, throwing it in the air to thunderous applause; the cheese sandwich next, gulped down, as with a flamboyant swirl of beating wings; and it descended a third time for the leg. Billy screamed with pain and the little wagtail flew off in fright. He had attempted to turn his body.

Derek, in a small room at the hotel, slept sporadically. He got up and read the note again. It seemed to have little relevance to the situation now. The hours dragged, his visions of Billy too frightening. At three a.m. he gave up his bed and dressed. Through the window he saw the night was dry and overcast. The clouds would keep the temperature higher, Derek thought, clinging to straws. He searched in vain for signs of sunrise. His room looked out on the ridge, the base of which was about a mile away. The sun would come up on his right and slant across the rocks, catching protruding rocks until it shone full blast at about seven. He used his phone and the hotel's wifi to watch the changing cloud formations and the projected weather to come. It would be fine. He found a crossword website and forced himself to concentrate; finished in ten minutes, he switched to chess. By four he saw the first light start in the east; it made the cliff rising about a mile away seem blacker and more ominous. He thought of a hospital corridor, the nights he had sat with Chris, nightlights turned down to a grey twilight.

He stepped carefully on floorboards and stairs, not wishing to disturb any who were catching sleep. Outside, the air was filled with a rising damp; the earth was returning that over-abundance of water, filling its cisterns for another day, and sunshine would soon comfort the living. The night was in retreat; yet on the hill it kept its still secrets shrouded. Derek began walking along a track that would lead to the old quarry and a route up a break in the escarpment — the same break Billy had hoped to find.

With the light came better thoughts — a day's sunshine and a full rescue team to find the boy. The top of the ridge showed clearly against the paler sky. Derek looked through binoculars; he saw where the Gargunnock waterfalls streamed down the steep rock. The falls looked still, just a white band in the dark immensity. He began his return to the car park, it would be getting on for five a.m. and Ken and the others would be down.

Although the sun had not appeared, it was significantly lighter and Derek turned once more to scan the rock. He knew that somewhere near the edge had been where the dog had lost Billy's scent. Light brought definition. Shades of green-grey differentiated scrub from bush; he stared through the lens centimetre by centimetre till his eyeballs ached. There was a fleck of colour — yellow gold, gorse in flower? He continued his panorama. Nothing. He returned the glasses to his pocket. Yet there was no other gorse in flower, it was sparse at this time of year, an odd branch retaining late bloom. There was no yellow anywhere else on the hillside. He looked again, and took his time, now beating back hope rather than dread. He found it, a tiny blotch of yellow. Hope now beating him, he ran the distance back to the hotel.

It was ten minutes to five and Ken was in the car park. Derek was breathless.

'I've found something on the hill, come along the track and look.' He turned and headed back along the track, Ken at his heels.

'Whit did ye see man?'

'Something. Some colour, it could be he's fallen.'

They were far enough along the track and Derek once more trained his glasses on the hill, it took him some minutes to find it.

'Look, Ken. To the left of the falls, can you see a bush, tree thing, sticking away from the rock? Just below that — a patch of yellow.' Ken strained for a few moments.

'Aye, Ah can see tha.'

'Well, it could be him.'

'A patch of yellow?'

'His coat or something?'

'More likely a patch of gorse.'

'But there isn't any anywhere else.'

Ken handed him back the glasses.

'We should go back. There's a bus collecting us to go up on the fell with the volunteers.'

'But what if…?'

'We can report what we've seen and mebbe the helicopter will get close enough tae check.' Derek hung back.

'C'mon man, we've got to be co-ordinated.'

'I'm going up, don't worry about me,' Derek said and started forward.

'I cannae stop ye, but fer God's sake take some provision wi ye.' Derek looked again through the glasses, he could find it easily now.

He would attempt it, foolish or not, but he would take provision.

The going was hard. He left the track, which would have taken him through the old quarry and onto the ridge, at a place where the undergrowth of stubby trees thinned enough to attempt a passage. He had no notion of a route other than to climb and keep heading towards the waterfall. It was a negotiation between horizontal and vertical. Once among the tangled branches of stunted hawthorn trees, he had little choice of direction. Once through, torn and scratched, he oriented himself to the waterfall and scrambled up over loose scree, slipping and bruising. Progress was slow, an hour had passed and he seemed scarcely to have risen at all. Confronted by sheer rock, he zigzagged back and forth to choose a fissure that he might climb.

The sun was up, slicing across the rock face. Inch by inch he made headway, his anxiety about the boy consumed in his mission to reach…what? A patch of yellow, a faith? Believing, like many zealots, the worse his travail the greater would be his reward.

Light registered behind Billy's eyelids, which he would block if he could so as to slip back inside and find his birds. If he could train the buzzard to take his leg he could crawl his way down the cliff. He was sweating and shivering. Each movement caused him piercing pain. He needed to bend his body so that his hands might reach the trunk. He imagined pulling the trunk to release the good leg and using that as a lever to drag out the other one. His success was microscopic, any further at one pull the pain would send him crashing back to his original position.

'Och, Ma!' he yelled, 'help me, Ma!' The river, because it was not his mother, took no notice.

At the crown of the fissure Derek rested, securing his feet and leaning into an outcrop of gorse. His legs were trembling from the exertion and he was breathless, stranded on a chimney of rock perhaps fifty metres from the top. No route, horizontal or vertical, suggested itself; and in any case he could not move until his legs stopped shaking. The gorse he was in had an occasional flower. He remembered a ridiculous saying, 'When the gorse is not in bloom then kissing is out of fashion'. But its full bloom was in March not August. He had not seen gorse blossom as Ken had suggested, but — despondent now — he thought it was equally unlikely to be Billy. He hunkered down to make himself more secure, found sweets and the binoculars in his pocket.

He leaned away from the cliff as much as he dared and scanned the terrain inch by inch, as much to find a way of safety for himself as to find his patch of yellow. A sculpted terrain of bush and rock, beyond which was the rising mist from the waterfall. The sun, as it moved round, spotlit areas in turn, as a film camera would survey the beauty of the cliff. He changed his position and looked back the way he had come up. Staring, disbelieving, below him to the left was a patch of yellow — some sort of plastic. It was fifteen difficult metres below him, impossible to see from below but now revealed. His heart was thudding. He steadied his position, and gazed at his object. Was it a yellow plastic waterproof? Something lost by a fell walker and blown down the rock? Or could it, just possibly, still be clothing its owner? Derek adjusted his position and concentrated on the spot; it lay below a dead tree that seemed to be an outcrop of the rock itself. It rested on gorse. His next mission was to get to it. It would take time but he could climb down the fissure he had ascended, cross the rock and scree and climb the one he had disregarded an hour ago.

The sun was getting higher; soon it would be full on the rockface. Dread accompanied his slow and careful climb. The top of this fissure was lower than the one he had been in, but he emerged into impenetrable gorse. It was impossible to know if there was solid rock or crevice beneath, and he could see no more than an inch or two into the tangle of vegetation. He shouted 'Billy' but his voice was weak against the water's roar. He had to clamber on top of the gorse and pull himself forward, disregarding the scratch and tear of it. A dip appeared ahead and, with one more pull, the yellow waterproof was visible. Visible also were the legs above it, twisted in a way that legs should not twist, between tree and rock.

'Billy, Billy!' Derek screamed as he pulled violently at the last yard of gorse. Billy lay still. Derek crawled to his side; he was white and no longer shivering, his eyes were closed, and he was freezing to the touch, but he was breathing. Short shallow breaths. Derek pulled all the spare clothes he had out of his bag, then took his jacket and jumper off, and covered Billy, fervently praying, to whatever deity was around, for a mobile signal. Crouching close to the ground, he pressed for Ken. He shouted slowly and at full throttle into the phone, and then he returned to Billy.

'We'll get you out of here, Billy.' There was no response and his breathing seemed even shallower. 'Billy. Wake up, look at me.' His eyes fluttered. He packed the clothes, more effectually around him, talking to him all the time and lay with his body next to him, as the sun beamed down upon them. Once he felt Billy tremble, his eyes flickered.

'Ma, whit ye doin' in ma bed? '

Derek cuddled him closer.

'Keeping you warm, son, just keeping you warm.'

It was half an hour before he heard the helicopter hovering above them; Derek removed himself carefully from beside the boy, replacing his own coat for the yellow waterproof, which he used to wave at the big bird that was stationary above them. At one point it flew north and Derek flapped and yelled, but it was only repositioning and soon he saw an umbilical cord drop from the guts of the bird. A man swung on the end, a metre above them; speech was impossible as the cacophony of engine and water throbbed. Derek pulled his way across the matted branches and guided the man down. Silently in the din they worked together, signing when necessary. Derek cradled Billy's head, now swathed in fleece, whilst the helicopter man sawed at the base of the tree that trapped his legs, and the big bird let down its line again with a stretcher. Billy was conscious.

'What's 594 times 56?' said Derek into his ear. There was no response. 'Well done, Billy, well done.'

The man signalled Derek to help. Gently they pushed the trunk, now half sawn, away from Billy's legs. They heard the scream above the din. The man prepared a syringe, to soothe the pain, before he took him swinging through the arc of a rainbow into the belly of his big bird.

Once more the line came down and the man indicated how they would strap themselves together for the lift. Derek shook his head and pointed down the rock. The man remonstrated, tried to grab Derek but there was nothing to be done without compliance.

Derek watched the dangling man re-enter the body of the helicopter and then began his own descent. Wearing only a T-shirt, he disregarded the scratches and cuts as he let himself be taken, only resisting gravity where the drop could be lethal, down, down, on talus, on rubble, through bush and gorse, with the waterfall receding and Billy on his way to Glasgow.

People were having lunch outside the Gargunnock Inn — he could see them from a distance as he approached. His T-shirt was in strips and bloody, his trousers were ripped, bruises on all visible skin. He would frighten the life out of the customers. He found a back door open and got to his room without being seen. He stood in the shower and watched the dirt and twigs mixed with blood swirl around the plughole. His body looked as though he had been in a serious fight; he turned up the heat, to disguise the smart of his wounds. He felt good. He had found Billy.

Wrapped in a towel, the warmth made him drowsy. He closed his eyes and let his mind wander. Billy playing Launcelot Gobbo. Billy at university. Billy a research assistant — Dr William Logan. A quiet knock on the door roused him.

'Derek, are you all right?'

It was a woman's voice. He had no clothes. He pulled the towel round his waist and sat on the bed.

'Yes, I'm fine.'

'We heard you found the boy.'

'Billy — yes, yes I did.'

'Won't you come down and have some food?'

'Er…I've got no clothes…they got torn, ruined really, on my way down.'

'I'll get you some, I'm Amanda by the way, I found your glasses up on the fell.'

There was clapping, from all in the garden of the hotel as Derek, in a borrowed tracksuit, approached. He blushed as he joined a group of rescue volunteers at a table. He hardly heard the babble of congratulations but accepted a pint, and a plate of fish and chips was ordered for him. Everyone wanted to know how he knew where Billy was, and how he had climbed the grim face of the escarpment, and how the boy was. The mood was quieter when it was clear that Billy's conditional was critical.

Gradually the group dispersed to their homes, in couples and singly. Only Derek and Amanda remained. She was a pretty woman in her forties, athletic-looking, with bobbed fair hair. Derek had only one lens left in his glasses after the return down the rock but through it he saw something of Chris. She wore no rings, maybe because of going on a search and rescue expedition. Derek said he was a widower; she said she'd moved up to Glasgow because of her partner's job, but they'd split up, he'd moved back to England and she had stayed. She loved the fells and came up every weekend; on longer breaks she'd go to the Highlands or down to the Lakes. She worked at the activity centre in Stirling and loved bringing groups of schoolchildren up here. He told her about his trip to the Hebrides, about losing Chris, that he was an English graduate, and the decision to come away from the sort of school in England where he taught.

They talked about walking, and climbing, and nature, and books, and poetry and in the bubble of their conversation Derek saw something.

Amanda drove Derek to Glasgow early the next day.

'I need to return your tracksuit.'

'There's no rush.'

'Should I post it?'

'You could, or why not drive up? We could have a walk and something to eat.'

'Yes, I'd like that.'

It was arranged for her next day off.

Back at his rented apartment, he changed. He made an appointment with a high-street optician. Then he set about finding out where Billy was.

The hospital was monolithic, grey, a hangover from previous prosperity. Between the rounded towers and the central fortification, row after row of tall narrow windows, set in the grey black stone. There were other, more modern 'temples to the sick' in the city but a phone call had told him that Billy was here, in the surgical high-dependency unit. Derek understood from his phone call that visits to this unit were usually limited.

Hospitals had become a regular part of his life as Chris's illness developed. Like city shopping malls, the layout of shops and cafés near the entrance was familiar. Shops selling presents for the inmates, flowers, food, cards. He wandered round and chose a packet of biscuits. The café in this one was open to the corridor and empty tables were piled with dirty crockery.

Nevertheless, he was hungry. He ordered a veggie burger and tea and cleared a table. The Friends of the Royal Glasgow Infirmary Art Group had donated the pictures on the walls. Hospitals, like airports, seemed to exist outside normal time. Derek was a bit like that anyway, all his props gone, no timetable, no work, no person to prove he was real. He thought about Amanda.

He took a lift to the surgical ward. A person in pyjamas was wheeled in. No eye-contact. He was of the sick domain, and Derek of the healthy outdoor world. Others came in and out, as the lift called at several floors, day or nightclothes defining their status.

At the ward all visitors were directed to a station where a nurse sat looking at a screen.

'Hello. Would it be all right to visit Billy Logan?'

'Are you a relative?'

'No.'

'Just a moment.'

The nurse went off in pursuit of higher authority. After a while a staff nurse appeared.

'It's really just relatives that visit here. His mum and his nan have been, and he is very tired. Do you mind telling me who you are?'

'Derek Baker, I was with the group on the fells. I found Billy and stayed with him until the helicopter came.'

'I see. Wait a moment.'

She returned quite soon and said that Billy would like to see him, but that he must stay no longer than five minutes. She directed him to his bed.

His bed was close to the nurses' station. He had two drips attached to his arms and a covered cage protecting his lower body from the bed covers.

'Hello Billy,' Billy smiled, 'I brought you some biscuits.' Derek put them on his side table. 'How are you feeling?'

'OK. Waz it youse there, on th' rock?'

'It was your yellow coat, it was like a beacon.'

'Ah remember. Then th' helicopter came.'

'That's right.'

'It waz thirty-three thousand, three hundred and thirty-four' Derek was flummoxed.

'The sum.'

'That's right, Billy.'

The boy looked pleased. After a while he closed his eyes. Derek stayed for a few more minutes, watching. The nurse was hovering.

'Good luck son, see you soon.' Derek squeezed his hand, thanked the nurse and left his bedside. Back at the station he asked what was happening to Billy.

'He'll have his operation tomorrow.' Derek looked questioning. She looked sympathetic. 'They'll do their best for him.'

Derek drove back to Cumbernauld that evening. He'd spoken to Ken, who had invited him to his flat for a beer.

'Come in, come in, sorry about the mess. Leslie always kept it spick and span, but try as I might, I cannae seem to manage it.' Derek had completely forgotten that way back Ken had said he was a widower.

'You never mentioned Leslie before.'

'Hae I not? She died, five years ago now.'

'I'm sorry.'

'Och weel, ye'll know all aboot that.'

Ken got two beers from the fridge in the kitchen, and invited Derek to sit on one of the two armchairs. They were covered in a beige fabric printed with big peonies. The flat was not particularly untidy and was in fact spotlessly clean. Ken put the beers and glasses on coasters on a coffee table and sat in the other armchair.

'Have ye recovered from yer climb?'

'More or less, just the odd scratch.'

'Ye did well Derek, finding him like tha'. Ah dinnae know how ye knew.'

'I didn't, it was sheer luck.' Derek told him the details of the rescue, and told him about the sum and the answer Billy had given him earlier in the hospital.

'Aye, the boy's got a gift.'

Ken got up to fetch more beer. 'Wud ye like something stronger?'

'No. I've got to drive back.'

'No need, there's a bed here, always made up.'

Derek thanked him but said another beer would be fine. While he fetched them, Derek found the note and spread it on the table.

'Whit's that?'

'I found it in the corner of the grouse butt where Billy had been. I was last in there because I dropped my glasses.'

Ken stood and read it and was silent for a while.

'Why did ye no' mention this before.'

'It was difficult to find an opportunity.'

Ken's famous eyebrows lifted a couple of centimetres.

'Unfortunately, Ah've got something tae show ye.' He fetched a laptop, opened it and put in an address and then handed it over.

The headline read:

'Boy lost on fells — English teacher with paedophile history in charge'

It took a moment for Derek to realise what it was he was reading… The article referred to a teacher who had recently been asked to resign from an English public school after an incident involving two boys. This was horrible. He was cold, colder than when he was with Billy on the fell. The sentence he had just read was the truth. He looked across at Ken.

'Ah think ye'd best take a drink, ye look very pale.' He fetched the whisky bottle, the general adult medicine for all complaints, and poured Derek a big one.

'They're bastarts, these journalists.'

'I should show the note, that's why he was running away.'

'The note should go tae the polis, tha's fer sure. Best do nothing aboot the article, if thair's nothin' to stoke it, it'll die. Maybe keep away from Cumbernauld for a wee while.'

He wanted to get rid of him?

'Run away again, you mean. I've done nothing wrong.'

'Ah ken tha'. Ah ken.'

They drank in silence. Ken sinking into the plumped red peonies, an oversized bee dusted with orange pollen; Derek, stick-like, hardly depressing the cushion.

'Billy's a good boy. He'll tell his ma how it waz, and the lads.'

'They've all read this?'

'One reads it, it gets out.'

'Ina?'

'Aye, she's bin doin' a bit of shoutin.'

'I was going to ask if I could get Billy a placement somewhere, you know, to make the most of his gift.'

'Aye, we've got that in hand. There's a sixth form college in Glasgae, he's been interviewed. When he's done his standards, and Ina is placated, he'll be aff, staying in a hostel all week. He'll be OK, that one.'

'And the court case?'

'We'll look after him… But don't forget, if youse hadnae climbed that rock, he very likely wouldnae be here. We know tha', Billy knows tha', and in the end Ina will know tha'. More whisky?'

In the morning Ken fried up a Cumbernauld special — two fried eggs, bacon, sausage, black pudding, haggis, tea and toast. Derek was feeling a bit sick.

'Och, laddie, ye need to put a lining on yer stomach.'

Ken was not that much older than Derek (five, maybe seven years) but 'laddie' seemed appropriate, and Derek didn't mind. He also found it was good advice and felt much better after his breakfast. Ken walked him to his car. A group of teenagers were hanging around, near his vehicle.

'Scram, yer young tykes,' Ken yelled. They ran and as they turned the corner of the flats one yelled 'Pervert!'

'Did they mean me?'

'Dinnae fash yersel', get off now, and keep in touch.'

On the third floor of a previously Council-owned property that was his new home, he unpacked. It didn't take him long, there wasn't much, and there wasn't much space. A decent-sized flat once, the present owner had created three flats out of one. There was a tiny kitchen (a 'kitchenette', he remembered they used to call them), he'd shared something similar with Chris back in his student days. The sitting room had an electric fire with a plastic cover representing coal, over a red light bulb, and two heating bars above, possibly illegal and also from the kitchenette era. The bedroom struggled to contain a three-quarter sized bed and a flimsy wardrobe. He set up his computer on the table in the sitting room. There was no contact from the old days, nothing from Max, just confirmation of a job interview at an agency on Monday and the usual spam. Next term was approaching; he could eke out his money until Christmas, but he really should get a job soon. He emailed his sister and gave her his new address.

He couldn't stop himself thinking about what was written about him on Cumbernauld media. He checked the papers to see if there had been any response, and was relieved to see that there had been none. It was surely fading to old news now. During the five days before he drove to Stirling, he visited Billy again but found he was post-operative and in intensive care so he was not allowed to see him. He walked around the city; he bought a new jumper, visited art galleries and museums and read in the evenings.

Finally, it was Saturday and the day held promise. He wore a new jacquard patterned jumper, matching his new specs. Amanda had suggested a hike; he took a small backpack containing some bottled water and a waterproof jacket, though the weather was set fine. The tracksuit had been washed at the local launderette and was now neatly folded in an Edinburgh Woollen Mills carrier bag, where he'd bought his jumper. The car needed diesel; he found a filling station and bought a breakfast sandwich and, although he would be too early, set off for Stirling. He was meeting her at the Sports Centre, after she finished her morning session at one p.m.

He was reading the *Guardian*, his coffee long finished, when she sat down opposite him.

'Gosh, I'm sorry, I'm late. Have you been here long?'

'Only an hour.'

'I thought we said one o'clock.' She sounded dismayed.

'That's right, but I didn't have anything to do so I thought I'd come over and have a look at the Centre. The café is lovely. I've brought your tracksuit.'

'Do you want to have some lunch here?'

'I don't mind.' He could not say that without remembering Max. 'Are you hungry?'

'I thought we were going for a walk so I packed us something.'

She was jittery, he shouldn't have been so early.

'Great, you're in charge,'

'I'll just get Toby from reception,' she said and turned so she didn't see his face fall. She returned with Toby, her Jack Russell terrier.

'They look after him in reception while I'm running sessions. Your car or mine?'

'I don't mind driving.'

'I'll do directions then. Great jumper by the way.'

They drove for about fifteen minutes and parked near a track.

'I know this hike it usually takes about three hours — is that OK?' Derek said it was fine and they set off. He had been worried that they might not find things to talk about but they chatted easily, about unimportant things, and after an hour stopped for their lunch. Amanda chose the spot, in a small cluster of trees with a fine view. It was well chosen, as considered as the lunch, which consisted of sourdough bread, tuna and hard cheese, peaches and a bottle of Alsace. She spread the picnic on a blanket, and sat cross-legged offering Derek the delightfully packed sandwiches. Derek, who said his legs were not meant to cross, found a tree stump to sit on. A group of small pines shaded them. The sun was hot, the food was good and the wine disinhibiting. They discovered that they liked the same music. There was a group playing in Stirling next weekend, maybe Derek could drive up again.

Amanda carefully repacked the lunch remains into her bag. Derek took the empty bottle in his. They both stood up at the same time and found themselves close. He placed his arms around her and they kissed.

'Shall we carry on? I mean, with the walk.'

'Yes, I'm ready,' Derek said, as he fumbled with the zip of his backpack.

Later, as they watched the sun go down through the small window of Amanda's cottage, Derek said, 'There have been some lies written about me on the internet.'

'I know.'

'You know?'

'Yes, there are always shits who like to dig up keech and always folk who want to tell you about it.'

'Keech?'

'Shite.'

'So you didn't believe it? You didn't mind?'

'I didn't believe it; but you can tell me about it if you want to, or not.'

Derek told her the sorry tale of Max, and Amanda said she thought he was a good man, and that in a real school that's how he would have been expected to behave. It was eight-thirty.0; the light was beginning to fade as it did in August this far north. She got up to feed Toby and make supper for them. They sat in the sweet-smelling garden, wrapped in blankets, and told versions of their life stories. On Sunday they slept late, read the papers, ate well and played endless games with Toby, who they sent to fetch the ball from the stream at the bottom of the garden until the poor dog was trembling with cold and over-excitement and had to be rubbed down and cuddled.

On the drive back, a local radio station was playing jazz. He turned it up. He muttered aloud: Amanda, Amanda; Amanda and Derek; my girlfriend Amanda. Was it too soon after Chris? Fuck it, he was happy and who was there to criticise? He drummed to the beat on the steering wheel, slid past mundane traffic in the slow lane. He would get a new car, perhaps a four-wheel drive that would go off-road. There was still some money and he'd get a job soon. He turned into the car park at the back of his block of flats and got out.

The blow was massive, violent, unexpected. It came from behind — he experienced it in slow motion, like a version of 'the human cannonball' he'd once seen at a circus in Switzerland. He felt himself projected and, as he watched from a high place, his face smashed into the concrete. In Switzerland, there was a soft landing, and anyway it was a trick.

'Fucking pervert.'

'Peedo.' A boot in the belly curled him into a ball; whilst a second, fractionally later, in the kidneys burnt him with unendurable pain. He had heard the words, before darkness descended; he understood.

The theatre was throbbing, crowds poured down wide curving staircases, lobbies resembling packed tube trains, emptying suddenly as if in a station, those leaving being immediately replaced. Getting to a bar was impossible and in any case the play was about to start. They joined a crush swarming towards an entrance marked 'stalls'. The crowd had its own momentum; most of its members were eyes down on mobile phones. Max too was absorbed by the tiny screen.

'It's like a satnav, it will take us to our seats,' Max said.

Derek kept close; they squeezed past endless people to their place in the centre of the row.

'Just in time.'

The old-fashioned curtain parted to reveal a painted backcloth of mountains and forests. It must be 'The Scottish Play', thought Derek. But the next night, and the theatre just as jam-packed as before, the crowd parted; Max was carried along the main lane, Derek forced onto a slip road. Once in the theatre, Derek found his seat, but strangely it faced the back of the auditorium. He turned, craning his face towards the stage. He could see Max in the seats they had occupied the previous night, and Amanda was sitting next to him, she turned and waved. Derek glanced at a neighbour's programme to see what play was being performed — 'Love's Labour's Lost.' The curtain parted and he found himself on the stage, he had no idea of the lines he should speak, someone was shouting his name, around him was the paraphernalia of an operating theatre.

'You OK, Derek? We'll get you back to the ward now, it's all gone very well. Tube feeding for a few days, I'm afraid.'

Rubber doors swung open, white walls, white uniforms, curtained cubicle. Arm constricted.

'Blood pressure's fine now, are you comfy?'

How could he know?

A day later, maybe — it was hard to tell (tube fed, drugs dripped, jaw wired) — there was a familiar face at the end of the bed. Eyebrows, broad red face. Derek couldn't smile; he lifted his hand, a sort of wave.

'Och man, they've made a mess of youse.'

Through a closed jaw, Derek tried to speak.

'Whit ye say?'

Derek fumbled for an iPad by his bed.

'Thanks for coming,' he wrote.

'Ah've bin every day.'

'What day is it?'

'Wednesday. Do you remember what happened?'

'It's coming back, but I've lost a couple of days.'

'They got the scum who did it.'

'Good.'

'They were caught running away. Polis on the beat, can ye imagine? Glasgae! Good job or ye might've bin kilt. Ah'm so sorry, Derek. Ah should've taken more care of ye.'

'I'm not one of your lads.

'Ah know, but this isnae the Home Counties.'

'Can you let Amanda know?'

'Aye, she knows.'

'Can you find me a mirror?'

'Ah'll see whit the polit bureau oot there has tae say.'

Derek, left alone, tried to feel his way round his face with his fingertips, difficult amongst the hardware and tubes and bandages. Ken returned with a senior nurse, Ken always had clout.

'You might be a bit shocked, but most of it is bruising and once the jaw is set and the stitches come out on your head you'll start to look like you again.'

The nurse handed him the mirror. He only had one eye to see the mess, and that eye was half closed. What was visible of his face was livid, his head totally bandaged and his jaw held in place by a massive brace. Derek handed the mirror back and wrote, 'Well if you are sure it's me, I'll have to take your word for it.'

Ken smiled. 'You're a guid man, Derek. They've got me down as next of kin. Should Ah change that fer yer sister?'

'No, not if it's no bother.'

'It's nay bother!'

'Och now, will youse look at you? Och. they made a real mess. Tha' must hae bloody hurt — did they get the boot in? Steel-caps? I seen youse on the telly, but it looks far woss now. They caught the young bastarts, probably them Lithuanians, who did it. Place is crawlin' wi 'em… Mind you, thair's a fair few Scots bastarts as well… Ah've bin visitin' ma own wee boy. He's a brave, clever lad is Billy. He said to visit ye, so here Ah

am. Ah've brought youse a wee dram to mak ye feel better.'
Derek indicated that he couldn't drink.

'Och weel, best not let it go tae waste. Ye got a wee paper cup, there's a guid man… Och tha's a nice wee drop… Ma Billy says ye helped him on the cliff, he says ye got the bloody helicopter there an tha'… They didna believe me when Ah told 'em down at The Crown tha' he'd got to bloody 'ospital in a bleedin' helicopter… Then tha' waz on the telly as well. I didnae know youse was wi' 'im… Ah was there… Ah seen ye in the mornin', an Ah thought ye wur away wi' the others… Ken's mate, Hugh, drove me to the hospital. Ma boy trussed up, oven-ready, Ah couldnae believe it, he might hae deed… Then this bloke in The Crown said aboot that stuff on t'internet, boot youse like… Well, I didnae want tae believe it, but it waz on the local news, ye know…that peedo stuff.'

Derek turned on his side away from her.

'Ah know, ah know, but ah didnae know then, like. The guys were getting pretty worked up…like you'd chased him off the cliff or sommat… Ah didnae know where you lived, it waznae-me who told… Ah know now…youse saved ma boy's life…an ye got beat up for it an' all… Ah ye sure ye willnae have a drink wi me? Ah could find youse a straw?'

Derek turned back. If he could have smiled he would have.

'Ma Billy's going to college, Ken says he can fix it… Ah wanted him to go down to Bec's, they were takin' people on… but be no use now… they want able-bodied… He's always bin a clever wee one, ma Billy. Ah dinnae know where he gets it from. Mebbe his da, he didnae stay around lang enough fer me to find oot. Anyways he'll come hame at weekends, and Ah'll still get ma allowance, Ken says'.

There was a wonderful scent — bluebells or maybe hyacinth. Derek had been sleeping, he breathed deeply, he couldn't get enough of the perfume. He was no longer in intensive care. The ward he was in had eight beds; he was at the end of a row, near a window; it was early evening and the sun in the west streamed through, making it difficult to recognise the person at the end of the bed — female, blonde, the sun making her hair golden, and the wonderful perfume. Fancifully he thought of angels.

'I've been waiting for you to wake up. With your scaffolding, I can't find anywhere to kiss you.'

Derek reached for his tablet and wrote, 'Just as well, I might have turned into a frog.'

'How are you feeling? Does it hurt still?'

'Getting better, the brace comes off next week, then they'll let me go.'

'Where to?'

'Back to the flat, I suppose? Job hunting.'

Derek had very little anchorage. Two people, Ken and Amanda, who hardly knew him, gave him some sense of belonging somewhere. If he went back to Birmingham and the patronage of his sister, he'd soon be just a Scottish anecdote. Perhaps that's how life is, a series of anecdotes.

'Sorry I missed the concert, how was it?'

'I didn't go.'

'How's Toby?'

'He's fine, they are looking after him at work, got to be back by ten. Thought I'd lost him a couple of days ago. Ken had called me and told me about you. I took him for a walk in the evening and I suppose I wasn't paying attention. Suddenly I realised I hadn't seen him for a while so I began calling. You know he usually comes, I was getting worried. Then I heard him bark; he seemed to be in a field next to the one I was in but it was impossible to see through the hedge, or for me to get through, and the barking had stopped so I thought maybe it wasn't him after all. I made wider and wider circles, calling and calling. Then I heard the bark again, back where I'd first heard it. When I got there, it had stopped.

Anyway, I found a way round into the next field but I found myself behind a deer fence. There was a strip of about three metres between the fence and the hedge, full of brambles and nettles. Then I heard him bark again, but now it sounded like he was back on the path on the other side, so I struggled back. Still no Toby, no bark. There was a small river nearby so I tried to see if he had crossed it, though he doesn't usually like water. Another bark and I knew he was the other side of the hedge and that he must be stuck. It was a relief of sorts, though it took me twenty minutes to negotiate a way between the deer fence and the hedge, and, with very nettled legs, to find him in a ditch directly alongside the hedge and too deep for him to scramble out.'

'Good old Toby.'

It was still early for visitors; Derek was up. With no drips, and a reduced brace, he could speak — after a fashion. Two more days the consultant had said, then he would remove the final scaffold and Derek could go home. He wandered out to the day room but the constant television drove him back into the ward. There was a wheelchair by the nurses' station. Four of them were gathered round and whoever it was, clearly a comedian, was punching the air and the nurses were convulsed. Derek passed.

'There he is. Derek, hang on, there's a friend of yours here.'

Derek turned around. The nurse turned the wheelchair round to face him. It was Billy; Billy in the wheelchair; Billy with one leg; why had no one had told him?

'Wow, youse look like a baboon's arse.'

'Well, you look a lot better than when I last saw you.'

'Except fer th' leg.'

'Yes, I didn't know about that. That's pretty bad luck.'

Billy swung the chair expertly round and they went to the day room together. As there was no one else there, Derek switched the television off.

'Mebbe bad luck, mebbe some good too. Anyways Ah'm awffy sorry Ah caused ye sae much bother. Ah shudn'ave ran aff like tha'. Ye saved ma life, Derek. Yer a guid man.'

Dear Amanda, it has been a long while and I hope that you are well. I occasionally get news of you from Ken. He told me you were running your own business now, 'Outward Bound for the City Bound.' Well done. I hope you don't mind hearing from me. After all we did part friends? I have moved schools a couple of times but am now settled in Edinburgh teaching final year English Literature in a new Academy. I still get out on the hills as often as possible, but this Easter finds me in Venice on a school trip with six of my students.

Venice has many memories for me, the last holiday with Chris when she was so ill, the production of The Merchant soon after she died, and how that was mixed up with the meetings with Ken and the gang. Dear Billy, an accountant now I hear, still looking after his mum and living in North Cumbernauld. Perhaps you will remember some of my stories, which is what prompted me to write. Although I have wanted to do so for some while.

It feels strange to find myself here again in Venice, seven years since Chris died and I moved to Scotland. Needless to say, my students have been studying The Merchant and earlier today, on a sight-seeing trip there was a very strange co-incidence.

We were on The Rialto Bridge, fighting our way through the hoards of tourists. We managed to get to the edge and stopped for a while to look over at the canal and talk about how Shylock would have done business there, when I heard an English voice behind me say:

'Tell me where is fancy bred,
Or in the heart or in the head?
How begot, how nourished?
Reply, reply.'

So, turning I spoke the reply:
'It is engendered in the eyes,
With gazing fed; and fancy dies
In the cradle where it lies.'
Standing before me, gazing as the verse describes was an extraordinarily beautiful young man.
'Mr Baker?'
'Max.'
We embraced, and laughed and couldn't speak for having so much to say. I introduced him to some of my students. He said he had to go as he had an appointment but we arranged to meet later.

I went alone to the café on Piazza San Marco, it was as crowded as I had expected. I looked around and caught an arm waving across the tables. He was looking out for me. On the table I noticed a small volume of poetry, together with a bottle of champagne. It was an immense pleasure to see him again. I grew so close to him in that first year after Chris, something I didn't understand at the time. Nothing was left of the awkward boy I knew, and yet his serious soul and deep thinking were revealed as he told me much about his life. He embarrassed me with thanks for my conversations with him when he was fourteen. He reminisced about time at St Edmunds but told me he only stayed on for one more term after I left. He persuaded his father to let him go to another school where he felt more 'at home'. He was at Cambridge now, as I predicted he said, and reading English. At this point another young man joined us, Max introduced him as his friend William. It was a completely joyous evening.

Today I visited the attractions of Venice with my group with renewed vigour, (despite the hangover) and knew I had been right to stay in teaching.

Dear Amanda, I hope you will forgive me and understand that I had no one to share this unexpected gladness with.

I would love to hear from you, if you ever feel inclined to write.

Derek

Published by Write Side Left Ltd
DT6 3AG
www.WriteSideLeft.com